"I'm be

Maggie continued, "What makes you think you can just send me a letter and make me move?"

"Clause seven, paragraph two," Karr said succinctly. "Equivalent housing."

"You call what you're offering equal to this? How about the aesthetic value of this apartment? You may not have any appreciation of charm or beauty, Mr. Elliot, but..."

"Oh, I wouldn't go that far," Karr drawled, his gaze resting appreciatively on her face.

Maggie gritted her teeth. "I know, you find it in women, not old buildings. Spare me the sexist views, please—I'm not interested!"

"Since when is it sexist for a man to find a woman attractive?" he said softly.

Dear Reader,

Welcome to the latest book in our HOLDING OUT
FOR A HERO series. Every month for a whole year
we'll be bringing you some of the world's most
eligible bachelors. They're handsome, they're
charming but, best of all, they're single! And as twelve
lucky women are about to discover, it's not finding
Mr. Right that's the problem—it's holding on to him!

Hold out for Harlequin Romance's heroes in coming
months... Look out in April for:

THE RIGHT KIND OF MAN
by Jessica Hart

Available wherever Harlequin books are sold.

Happy reading!

The Editors
Harlequin Romance

Some men are worth waiting for!

The Only Man for Maggie
Leigh Michaels

Harlequin Books

TORONTO • NEW YORK • LONDON
AMSTERDAM • PARIS • SYDNEY • HAMBURG
STOCKHOLM • ATHENS • TOKYO • MILAN
MADRID • WARSAW • BUDAPEST • AUCKLAND

For Dianna—
lovely lady, generous woman,
precious friend.
Thanks for being there.

ISBN 0-373-03401-6

THE ONLY MAN FOR MAGGIE

First North American Publication 1996.

CHAPTER ONE

MAGGIE Rawlings looked out the window of the taxi at the soft green haze that clouded the bushes alongside the narrow highway, and sighed in contentment. A month ago, when she'd left, it was still winter. Now spring had spread promise across the land.

"It's good to be home," she said, almost to herself.

The driver glanced from one side of the road to the other, and then cast an incredulous look at her in the rearview mirror. "Home?" he said. "Where?"

Maggie laughed. Even though they were just a mile from the nearest town, the place *did* look like the outside of nowhere to a stranger's eyes—a twisting country highway without a building in sight, just a ramshackle wrought-iron gate off to one side of the road. "It doesn't look like much, does it? It's impossible to see the house from here. You don't need to go all the way in. Just drop me at the gate, please."

The cab slowed. "You mean *this* gate?"

Maggie was already gathering up her possessions— the leather briefcase, which held the laptop computer that went everywhere with her, the soft-sided weekend bag, the brightly colored pizza box. She paused with her hand on her wallet and studied the gate in question.

Maggie could understand the cabby's skepticism. It had been a long time since she'd really looked at the gate, and familiarity had worked its softening magic. Now she saw that the wrought-iron archway leaned even more than it had when she'd last paid attention, and one gate was hanging askew from a broken hinge as if someone had run a car into it while she'd been gone. Not that it mattered, really. Maggie didn't know anyone who remembered the last time the gate had actually worked. But the wrought iron was old, solid and intricate, and despite the damage it was still beautiful.

"This very gate," she said firmly, and slid out as soon as the cab halted. She slung the computer case over her shoulder by its strap, set the weekend bag down on the verge of the road and balanced the pizza box on top while she tugged an assortment of bills out of her wallet. The worst thing about living at Eagle's Landing was the cost of getting home from O'Hare Airport, she thought philosophically.

The cabby surveyed Maggie slowly and thoroughly, his eyes roving over her slim, angular body and appraising her clothes. Her tweed jacket and tailored wool slacks were a bit crushed from her long flight, but the look in his eyes said that even when she was crumpled from travel, Maggie Rawlings looked better than average.

"I had you figured to live in one of those new condo developments," he confided. "Woman like you—all style and polish and with looks like a model—it doesn't seem right for you to live at the end of nowhere."

"Well, everyone miscalculates now and then," Maggie said coolly. She added a tip and held out the cash.

The cabby counted it thoughtfully. "You know, I'm supposed to get three times the amount on the meter for trips this far out in the sticks."

"And mistaking me for a greenhorn is your second miscalculation," Maggie added. "Of course, if you'd like me to take it up with the transit authority, I'll be happy to give them the number of your license."

"I'm just trying to make a living," he grumbled, and pulled away so fast that the smell of burning rubber hovered in the air.

Maggie shook her head. Why, she wondered, did so many men believe that if a woman's face and figure weren't hard on the eyes, she had no brain worth mentioning? Though perhaps it was no wonder they thought that, for even the smartest of women could be incredibly gullible sometimes. Maggie had been, once—and she was still paying for it three years later.

She picked up her bag and the pizza and started up the drive. It was long, narrow and curving, and a pleasant walk after the hours she'd spent sitting in an airplane. Along the edges of the road the green spikes of daffodil leaves poked through the rich cool earth in dense clumps. There were fewer of them this year than in the previous two springs when Maggie had watched the garden stubbornly come to life. But then no one paid much attention to the flowers any more.

Maggie rounded the corner, and the house called Eagle's Landing came into view. It was a tall, slate-roofed Tudor revival mansion, so perfectly proportioned that it was hard to believe how enormous it really was. The earth-brown brick walls and deep green slate roof blended perfectly into the landscape, and the dark timbers and cream-colored stucco accents that trimmed the top two floors made it look like a gigantic gingerbread house with its narrowest side facing the drive. It looked as if it had always been there—as if it had simply grown, like the mature oaks and maples that nestled around it.

Maggie couldn't help smiling at the sight. The house was unusual, full of fascinating idiosyncracies—so different from the plain, perfectly rectangular apartments where she'd lived before. That fact alone would be worth the time and money she spent commuting, even if the rent hadn't been low enough to compensate.

It was just as well she hadn't asked the taxi to take her to the door, because the side entrance was blocked by a contractor's van. A tall ladder leaned against one of the chimneys, and at the very top, a man poked at the intricate brickwork with some sort of tool.

From the ground, Maggie couldn't see what he was doing. Odd, she thought, that the owners would be fussing with the chimneys. None of the tenants used the fireplaces any more. In fact, they'd been blocked off long before Maggie moved in. She'd have thought the landlords would be more interested in improving the water pressure. That had been the subject of the last letter the tenants had sent, just the week before Maggie had left on her business trip.

That was the difficulty with absentee owners, she thought. If they'd been occupying one of the dozen apartments themselves, she'd bet there wouldn't be any lack of water pressure.

She gave a philosophical sigh. At least there weren't a lot of problems at Eagle's Landing—though the credit for that went to the manufacturing baron who had built the house so solidly in the first place, not to the current owners for their maintenance policy.

She nodded politely to the two workmen on the ground at the base of the ladder and went in the side entrance. The hallway was dim, as it usually was on even the brightest days, since the doors to all the rooms were closed and the only natural light crept through the beveled glass in the front and side doors.

Sometimes Maggie wondered what the house had looked like when it was new, when a single family lived here and light and air had circulated freely through the whole house. But now the two big drawing rooms were a separate apartment, and the old dining room and kitchen formed another, and the library and music room were yet a third—and so the doors were always closed to give privacy to the renters.

Her own apartment occupied the entire top floor. It was the largest and in Maggie's view the most luxurious apartment in the entire house. Fortunately for her, few people agreed with her that the sheer space made up for the lack of an elevator, so her rent had remained reasonable.

As usual, she was breathing a little harder than normal by the time she reached her door. But as soon as she turned the lock and pushed the door open, she forgot the climb and the weight of her bags in pure enjoyment of space and light.

The apartment was more like a loft. It was one huge room with windows on all four sides, tucked into the high-pointed gables—so even in the most oppressive heat she always had a breeze, cooled by the rustling trees. The ceiling followed the irregular steep slopes of the roof, extremely high in the center peak but so low in the corners that Maggie could hardly stand straight. The variations of the wings and gables formed odd nooks and angles, which gave the illusion of separate rooms. And when it rained, the patter of water drops on the slates formed a lullaby.

Before Maggie had ever seen the place, the rental agent had warned her that the apartment was unusual. It predated the transformation of the rest of the house into rental units, since it had been set up originally for a grown son who had wanted his own space. "He was very eccentric," the rental agent had almost whispered. "In fact, I understand he was downright odd."

Perhaps she was right, but the unknown, long-gone son had been Maggie's kind of odd. She'd known it the moment she'd walked into the apartment and saw the worn oak floors, the faded chintz curtains, the deeply carved mantel and the bookshelves on each side of the fireplace. She hadn't even bothered to check the kitchen and the bathroom. She'd signed the lease on the spot, and thanked her guardian angel that she'd been able to find something so unusual for so little money. Of course it would be nice to have more water pressure—but overall the quiet, the space and the view from her windows more than made up for the mechanical details.

The apartment smelled damp and musty from being shut up for four long weeks, so Maggie dropped her bags right inside the door, set the pizza box on the kitchen counter and went to open all the windows. The outside air was growing brisk as evening approached. It wouldn't take long to banish the stale smell.

She heard the ladder rasp against the slate roof as it was removed from the chimney, and wondered once more what that was all about. It was an unusual time of year to be checking the heating system, that was sure.

On the small drop-leaf table in the kitchen nook was a stack of mail. Maggie flipped idly through it. It was mostly junk. There was nothing that couldn't wait till tomorrow. She changed her low-heeled pumps for walking shoes and went down a floor, to the apartment that had once been the master bedroom and nursery. But there was no answer to her knock. The neighbor who always looked after Maggie's plants and her dog while she was gone must have taken Tripp for a walk, or else the Yorkie would have heard her by now and be raising Cain.

The air had cooled even more in the few minutes she'd been inside, and the sun had dropped noticeably. The workmen were obviously getting ready to leave. As Maggie left the house, the man who'd been inspecting the chimney was leaning into the back of the contractor's van, and the other two were lifting sections of the ladder to the rack on top of the vehicle.

Maggie paused. "Is something wrong with the chimney?"

The man inside the van didn't turn around. "A lot of loose brick inside. Nothing else that I could see."

His voice was like molasses on a warm day—rich and soft and deep, with a husky undertone that made him sound as if he'd just woken up. He was utterly wasted on a construction job, Maggie thought. He ought to be in radio. With a bedroom voice like that, even if all he did was read the Chicago telephone book, he'd have the highest ratings in the business.

"Is it going to collapse on some unlucky passerby anytime soon?" Maggie's tone was a little crisper than normal.

He drew his head out of the van and turned to face her, a toolbox in one hand. He was a bigger man than he'd looked atop the ladder. The sheer size of the house must have diminished him. But in fact he was a good eight inches taller than Maggie, who was no Pygmy herself. His shoulders were broad enough to strain the dark blue T-shirt he wore, and she could see the ripple of muscles in his arms and chest as he set the heavy box down.

His eyes were the precise shade of the T-shirt. Maggie wondered if he'd chosen the shirt for that reason, or if the color was reflected. His jeans fit like a second skin, but with the ease of long wearing and multiple washings, not vanity. His hair was light brown, a little too long and kissed with blond streaks as if he spent a lot of time in the sun. His face was tanned, and just craggy enough to be interesting rather than conventionally handsome....

She didn't realize she was staring until he smiled and said lazily, "Well, hello, there."

Not radio, Maggie decided. Give him a television show, and women would not only cancel every other engagement on their calendars to watch the tube, they'd wait in ticket lines for weeks in order to be part of the studio audience. Not, of course, that Maggie Rawlings would be among them. Recognizing a man's attraction was one thing, but letting it mess up her judgment was another, and she wasn't about to make that mistake again.

He was looking her over pretty closely too. The cabby's almost leering inspection had annoyed Maggie, but it hadn't upset her—she'd run into his kind before. In contrast, this man's appraisal made her uncomfortable in a much more elemental way, as if her internal thermostat had suddenly gone awry and her blood was growing warmer by the moment.

His gaze returned to her face, and Maggie braced herself for some kind of slick line. She'd asked for it, of course—approaching him like that. But whatever he said, she would put him promptly and firmly in his place and move on without giving him a chance to follow up.

The corner of his mouth curved up slightly, as if he'd read her mind and had no intention of playing by her expectations. "I shouldn't think it's likely. Do things collapse on people's heads a lot around here?" he asked.

Maggie had to pull herself together before she could even remember what he was referring to, and before she'd found her voice his smile had turned into a full-fledged grin, complete with a mischievous sparkle that made his eyes appear an even brighter blue.

That was quite enough of that, Maggie thought. It was past time to remind him that he wasn't there to flirt with the residents. "Not chimneys, at least," she said crisply. "The water pressure, on the other hand, is always falling at the least convenient moments. I hope the owners suggested you do something about that."

He shook his head regretfully. "Not a word about the water, I'm afraid."

"Pity," Maggie said. "I suppose the tenants' association will have to write another letter." She gave him a dismissing nod and crossed the drive toward the wooded area that stretched down to a little lake at the far end of the property. She was uncomfortably aware that he did not immediately return to work but stood easily with one hand propped against the open back door of the van, watching her. At the far edge of the driveway she turned to face him once more, hoping to discourage him with a disdainful look of her own. "By the way," she said coolly, "I do not appreciate being rudely stared at."

The rebuke bounced off him. "Oh, I wasn't staring rudely. My mother taught me never to do that. I was just enjoying the scenery—and you must realize you're well worth a second look. Besides, if you weren't doing a little observing of your own, how did you know I was watching?"

Maggie refused to dignify that remark with an answer. She spun on her heel, swinging a curtain of blue-black hair over her shoulder, and stalked away.

He laughed, and Maggie's blood grew even warmer. Life might be easier, she thought, if she gave up femininity altogether. Perhaps if she cut off all her hair and dressed in shapeless tents and horn-rimmed glasses...

A shrill bark ripped the air, and a small bundle of brown fur flashed out from among the trees and flung itself at Maggie, yipping madly. She bent over, trying to pat the Yorkie, but the wiry little body was in nonstop motion, tail wagging frantically, tongue swiping at anything that might be his mistress's fingers. Finally Maggie got a hand under the dog's stomach and picked him up, but even with all four legs off the ground Tripp wriggled as if he was running, and twice he nearly twisted out of Maggie's hands as he lapped at her face.

"What a darling," she cooed as she stroked his silky fur. "I've missed you, too, precious. And wait till you see what I brought you from a doggy boutique in San Francisco—"

"You know," the construction worker called, "this is the first time I've ever seen a toupee get so excited to see someone."

Maggie glowered at him. Her Yorkie was small and shrill and wildly enthusiastic, and Maggie might sound silly for talking to him as if he was a baby—but calling Tripp a toupee was going a bit too far.

A woman in her mid-thirties came out of the shadow under the trees. "Maggie! Thank heaven you're home!" She cast a look of pure dislike at the construction worker, seized Maggie's arm and pulled her away as if she'd been standing atop a nuclear waste dump. "You haven't been talking to him, have you?"

The construction worker grinned.

Maggie's eyebrows soared. "What happened, Libby?" she asked as soon as they were inside the house. "Did he give you an up-close-and-personal inspection, too? I should have remembered it's useless to try to put that kind of Neanderthal in his place. He probably treats every woman that way."

"Not me."

"Oh? Then why did you give him that look of intense distaste, as if he's done something unforgivable? Did he kick Tripp?" Maggie stopped in the middle of the hall, poised for a further confrontation. If that...person...had assaulted a helpless dog—

Libby shook her head impatiently. "Oh, it's nothing like that. Not that I'd blame the dog for biting one of them, but it's not the workmen's fault, they're just the flunkies. They're just *here*, you see, and it's getting on everyone's nerves. The ones who are left, I mean."

Maggie frowned. Libby usually wasn't quite this incoherent. "Would you tell me what the heck is going on?"

Libby's eyes widened. "Don't you know? Haven't you read your mail yet?"

"I just got home ten minutes ago. Which reminds me, I brought a pizza, and it's getting very cold. Do you and Dan want to come up, and we'll sort this all out over dinner?"

"I'll come, but Dan's working overtime. I hate having him gone all the time, but heaven knows we'll need the money." She started up the first flight of steps.

Maggie lagged behind. "Is that an announcement?" she asked carefully.

"Of what?"

"Well, I thought maybe you were telling me there was going to be a little Montgomery, after all."

"Not a chance." Libby sounded impatient.

That was strange. Normally, any turn of conversation that reminded her of the baby she couldn't seem to have would bring Libby to the brink of tears. Whatever had taken her mind off that problem must be a difficulty of enormous dimensions, Maggie thought. Well, it could wait another couple of minutes. The busybody who lived in the second-floor back was, as usual, peeking around the edge of her door and trying to overhear every word.

Inside the top-floor apartment, Tripp scrambled for his water dish and waited impatiently while Maggie filled it. She shivered a little and closed the kitchen windows. "I guess I did too good a job of airing the place out. This is the kind of evening when I wish the fireplace worked. Wouldn't it be nice to curl up beside a roaring blaze?"

Libby didn't answer. She went straight to the kitchen table and started sorting through the stack of letters while Maggie closed the rest of the windows. "I thought I left it on top so you'd see it right away."

"I dug through the pile and probably mixed it all up. I didn't find anything I thought was important, though. What's going on?"

Tripp slurped the entire dish of water and flopped on his belly on the rug in front of the kitchen sink, as if to say it was nice to be home. It was his favorite spot in the whole apartment—largely, Maggie was convinced, because he was most in the way there. She dug his new chew toy out of her handbag and offered it to him. Tripp surveyed it suspiciously for a moment, then dragged it back to his rug and lay down with his chin atop the bone-shaped chunk of rawhide.

Libby held up an envelope. "Here."

Maggie stepped over the dog to get to the oven. "Let me just stick the pizza in to warm first. I'm starving."

She came back to the table and took the letter out of Libby's hand. It was an ordinary business envelope, with the return address—Elliot Development Corporation—printed in the corner. She'd missed it because it looked like a typical direct-mail offer to sell her something she neither wanted nor needed, but now that she looked at it more closely, the name sounded vaguely familiar.

"What's Elliot Development, anyway?" she asked.

"The people who built the row of town houses on Westfield Drive, and the condo development along Rock Road, and the enormous apartment block on Elgin Avenue—"

"Aren't those the apartments that used to be a warehouse?"

Libby nodded.

"Now it just looks like a prison with a bad facelift. Are they trying to take over the whole city of Eagleton or what?" She turned the envelope over. "You haven't even opened this, Libby. How do you know what it is?"

"Everybody in the building got one."

"What are they trying to sell? The condos?" Maggie reached for a knife and slit the envelope. "You know, the cabby who brought me home from O'Hare thought

I was the condo type. If he'd known me any better, I'd have taken it as an insult."

Inside the envelope, instead of the brightly colored brochure she'd half-expected, was a single page of stationery. A personal letter, in fact, informing Miss Margaret Rawlings that Elliot Development Corporation had purchased the house and property known as Eagle's Landing and was invoking clause seven, paragraph two of the lease agreement to notify her that she had thirty days to vacate her apartment....

Maggie's fingers went numb, and the paper slipped from her hand. Tripp raised his head to watch it flutter to the floor, decided it wasn't interesting enough to chase and put his chin down on his toy.

"I'm being evicted?" she said shrilly.

"We all are. I told you, everybody got letters."

"They can't do that!"

"They've done it, Maggie."

"But it's not legal. We've got leases!" She'd signed a new one almost a year ago—but where had she filed the darned thing?

"It doesn't matter. Dan's read the whole lease a dozen times, and that clause says they can."

"That's utterly ridiculous! What's the good of having a lease if the landlord can pitch you out at the merest whim?"

"It's not exactly a whim," Libby said. She sounded as if she was making a great effort to be fair. "The clause says if it's necessary to end the lease early, the landlord will offer equivalent housing."

"Like what?" Maggie said suspiciously.

"Choice of the town house development or the condos—"

"That's what Elliot Development considers equivalent to this?" Maggie flung a hand out as if to encompass the entire room.

Libby smiled for the first time since Maggie had come home. "Or the prison-block apartments, if you'd prefer."

Maggie didn't bother to comment on that. "At the going rate, I suppose. What do those things cost, anyway?"

"Actually, that's the one thing they're being decent about—for the remaining period of the lease, the rent will be no more than we're paying here. Afterward, when the existing lease is up, it'll be negotiable—"

"Which is to say, higher."

"Of course. That's why Dan's working tonight, and every minute he can. It's not a bad deal, and our lease has another ten months to run, but—"

"I've only got two," Maggie said gloomily.

"That's a tough break. At least we're lucky to have some breathing room. But we don't want to have to move a second time, you see, so we need to save up a down payment so we can buy the town house and never be put in this situation again."

Maggie stared at her in utter disbelief. "You can't mean you're going along with this!"

"I don't see that we have a choice. Mr. Kelly downstairs is already gone, and Mrs. Harper is moving tomorrow."

Maggie shook her head. "I can't believe you're all being such wimps."

"You do have to look at it from their point of view," Libby said reluctantly. "Mr. Kelly can't drive any more, and Elliot's apartment block is within walking distance of downtown. And you know Mrs. Harper's air-conditioning gave her all kinds of problems last summer and it's not fixed yet—so I can't blame her for looking forward to a condo that's nice and new."

"And full of construction bugs to be worked out," Maggie said direly. "Believe me, I know all about those.

All right, I can see why some of the tenants might think it's a good deal. But they could at least have waited till the time was up before they caved in.''

"It *is* up, Maggie. The last day of the month is next Wednesday. We've got less than a week."

"It says thirty days!" Maggie scrambled to pick up the letter. "Right here—"

"And it's dated more than three weeks ago."

Maggie stared at the letter, then looked at Libby. "You didn't let me know?"

"Maggie, nobody knew for sure where you were! You sent postcards from California, Maine and Florida, but you never put a return address on them."

"And you didn't think of calling the magazine? I checked in with the office every few days."

Libby's eyes widened. "Oh. That was dumb of me, wasn't it? No, I honestly didn't. I was so stressed out I just didn't think."

Maggie supposed there was no point in making a fuss about it, because the damage was done. Or perhaps it wasn't—the fact that she hadn't gotten the full notice period might end up working to her advantage. "It doesn't matter now. We can still fight this. Just stand firm, Libby, and don't agree to anything."

"I don't know," Libby said doubtfully. "Dan sort of wants things settled, and so do I. I mean, it would be nice to know what our address will be next week."

Maggie wasn't listening. She was scanning the rest of the letter, absorbing the details she had been too stunned to notice before. "It doesn't say anything about why they want this place," she observed.

"I shouldn't think they'd have to tell us."

"Even though they're throwing us out? What *does* Elliot Development want with Eagle's Landing, anyway? A hundred-year-old house split into a dozen apartments is hardly their kind of property."

Libby shrugged. "Nobody seems to know. The workers who are hovering around don't have much to say."

Maggie thought of the one she'd encountered and muttered, "Not about that subject, anyway. As far as other things are concerned—"

"I should think by now you'd be used to male whistles, Maggie. Mr. Kelly tried to get hold of the previous owners, but they're out of the country."

"Spending the proceeds of the sale, I suppose."

"No doubt. And the people at Elliot Development were willing to talk about everything except their plans. Dan even called Mr. Elliot himself, but all he'd say was something about a great demand for upscale housing."

"That's it? 'A great demand for upscale housing'?"

"I think that's what Dan said."

Maggie sniffed resentfully. "So they want us to take up space in their precious condos instead of living here? Oh, that makes a lot of sense." She sniffed again, more deeply, and leaped up, knocking over her chair in her haste to get to the oven. Smoke seeped from it and billowed out in a cloud the moment she opened the door. On the oven rack lay the blackened ruin of her pizza, twisted and charred.

"That does it," Maggie said under her breath. "That's the last straw. It's bad enough that this development person—what's his name?"

"Karr Elliot," Libby said helpfully.

"Now he's not only trying to throw me out of my home, but he's ruined my dinner, too. And I'm going to see that he answers for it!" She dumped the smoldering pizza in the garbage and went straight to the telephone.

"I think I've got some TV dinners in the freezer. Maybe I'll just run down and pop a couple in the microwave."

"Are you too chicken to stick around? Libby, I'm only going to call the man. I probably won't even shout much."

But Libby had already vanished. Maggie flipped the directory pages till she found Elliot Development. When a woman answered the telephone, Maggie asked if Karr Elliot was in.

"Who's calling, please?" the receptionist asked.

"Does it make a difference?" Maggie asked sweetly. "I should think either he's in or he's not, and who I am shouldn't change that fact."

The receptionist was unflustered. "He's not."

Maggie glanced at her watch. Tomorrow would do well enough. In fact, it might even be better. She could look up her lease tonight and read that clause for herself so she'd be better prepared. "Tell him Margaret Rawlings called. In case he doesn't recognize that I'm one of his new tenants at Eagle's Landing, you might mention that I'm also the associate editor of a magazine called *Today's Woman*, and I'm quite interested in the way he's going around illegally breaking perfectly valid leases."

"I'm sure you'll be hearing from him soon, Miss Rawlings."

"You know, I'm sure of it, too," Maggie murmured. She put down the phone and dusted her palms together. That, she thought, should make Mr. Hot-Shot-Developer Elliot sit up and take notice. She'd think all her arguments out tonight, and tomorrow morning when he called...

She tried to ignore the twinge of panic at the pit of her stomach. She'd find a way to get around this—she had to. There weren't many places she could live as inexpensively as at Eagle's Landing, and she needed that financial edge right now. Two more years and she'd have her debts repaid and her head above water again. But right now...

She put the teakettle on and unpacked her weekend case. It wasn't much of a job, for she'd taken the bare minimum for her long trip, and almost everything needed to go to the cleaners. She'd just finished washing out her lacy undies and hanging them up to dry in the bathroom when there was a knock on her door.

Maggie glanced at her watch. That would be Libby, no doubt, with her hands full, trying to carry a couple of hot TV dinners. The woman really was a sweetheart, always trying to cheer up a friend even when she felt rotten herself.

Maggie flung the door open. "Come on in—"

Then she realized that it was not a petite young woman on the landing but a tall, broad-shouldered construction worker in a dark blue T-shirt and jeans.

She stared at him, mouth open. He wasn't smiling yet, but though Maggie hadn't known him long, she had no trouble recognizing the signs of his dawning amusement—his eyes had started to sparkle wickedly, and the corners of his mouth twitched.

"Now come on," she said heatedly. "If you think I was issuing an invitation to get better acquainted—"

"Oh, but you did, Miss Rawlings." He swept her a bow, a courtly gesture that was surprisingly graceful, considering the jeans and T-shirt. "I'm Karr Elliot, and you asked to speak to me specifically. Now, just what is it you wanted, I wonder?"

CHAPTER TWO

THIS man was Karr Elliot? The head of the biggest development company in town went around looking like a common laborer?

Well, maybe not exactly *common*, Maggie reflected. Any man with his height, broad shoulders, impressive muscles and level gaze could never be called common. Given time, she could no doubt come up with a few other appropriate adjectives—but he wasn't common.

"You know," she said tartly, "you could have told me who you are."

His eyebrows climbed. "Why? I'm not in the habit of announcing myself. If you'd wanted to know my name, you could have asked. Women often do that."

"I'll bet they do," Maggie muttered. She could almost feel sorry for them, deluded creatures—thinking that any man who was so good-looking must have a personality that was just as attractive. Maggie knew better.

"And since at the time I didn't know who you were," he went on logically, "I didn't see any reason to introduce myself. For all I knew, you could be a perfume distributor making your regular rounds—not one of my tenants at all."

Maggie decided there was no point in pursuing that subject. "What were you doing up on the chimney, anyway?"

"Taking a look at my new property."

"I expected you'd have inspectors and engineers to do that sort of thing."

"I do, but now and then I like to have a look for myself."

Maggie shook her head. "Don't your employees think that's sort of strange?"

"On the contrary. They seem to respect the fact that I don't mind getting my hands dirty."

As if the mere word was a magnet, her gaze dropped to his hands, resting easily on narrow hips. If she'd looked at his hands before, Maggie realized, she'd have known there was something out of sync about this man, for his hands didn't match his clothing. They were big, strong and well-shaped, with long fingers. But while they showed the marks of physical work, they weren't the hands of a laborer. There was no grime ingrained around the nails, which were well-shaped and cared for....

"Would you like a closer look?" he said mildly, and held out both hands as if for a parental inspection. "I washed them before I came upstairs."

Maggie was embarrassed to be caught staring, but she wasn't about to admit it. "Just as your mother taught you, I suppose."

"Of course. And I wiped my feet, too. So may I come in?"

It wasn't very polite to keep him standing in the hallway, and being rude would do her cause no good. Unwillingly, Maggie took a step backward. "Would you like a cup of coffee?"

He didn't seem to notice the reluctance in her tone. "That would be great."

Maggie waved a hand toward a pair of sofas, arranged at an angle on an Oriental rug that marked off the apartment's sitting area. "Make yourself comfortable while I fix it."

But Karr Elliot didn't immediately sit down. Instead, he remained standing in the foyer area, looking around the room. With evening coming on and the immense oak

tree on the west side of the house blocking the setting
sun, the corners and the upper reaches of the high ceilings
had grown shadowy, and the room looked even more
vast than usual. That impression was increased, Maggie
knew, by the sparsity of her furniture. The couches, the
library table that served as her desk, a couple of repro-
duction Oriental rugs, a pair of chairs that were more
comfortable than elegant, an enormous antique wardrobe
and her bed—that was about it. The only things she had
in abundance were houseplants and books. Greenery occupied every window, and the books filled the shelves
and the mantel.

The floor creaked under Karr's weight as he crossed
the room, and instantly his attention was focused on the
random-width oak boards beneath his feet. "Doesn't that
sound drive you mad?" he asked. "It's like fingernails
on a blackboard."

Maggie shrugged. "It's part of the charm of an old
house. Besides, I'm smaller than you are, so the floor
doesn't creak when I walk on it."

Immediately, she regretted calling his attention to her,
as that deep blue gaze once more traveled slowly over
her from head to foot and back. She wouldn't have been
surprised, when the appraisal was over, if he could have
calculated her weight to the ounce.

But he merely said, with an ironic note in his voice,
"Creaking floors and leaky roofs—oh, yes, old houses
are so charming." He sat down and tipped his head back
as if to study the peak of the ceiling directly above him.

The teakettle was whistling. Maggie spooned coffee
into a filter and poured the boiling water slowly over it.
"If you're not charmed by old houses, why did you buy
one?"

He didn't take his eyes off the ceiling. "To the best
of my recollection, it seemed a good idea at the time."

"That means you think it's none of my business."

"Well, the last time I looked, your name wasn't on my list of financial backers, so—"

"Never mind. The roof doesn't leak, by the way. At least it's never dripped on me. Why are you worried about it, anyway?"

"Did I say I was worried? It was merely an observation. There's so much damaged slate up there I'm astounded to hear it doesn't leak like a sieve." He appeared relaxed, his legs sprawled, but his gaze was moving steadily over the entire room. Maggie was willing to bet he wasn't missing a thing, from the deep carving on the walnut mantel to the mismatched antique chairs pulled up to her kitchen table.

She set the tray on the hassock, which sometimes doubled as a coffee table. Tripp, who had followed her from the kitchen, sniffed warily at Karr's boots and finally settled directly under Maggie's feet, still eyeing the newcomer.

"Haven't you inspected this part of your new property before?" she asked.

Karr shook his head without looking at her. "You were out of town, and your lease specifies that the landlord can't have access without your permission. Except for emergencies, of course—but buying the property didn't seem to fit that classification."

"You amaze me." She filled a mug for him. "I've got sugar, but I didn't pick up any milk, I'm afraid."

"That's fine. On construction sites you learn to drink coffee however you can get it." He accepted the mug and took a long swallow, heedless of the almost-boiling liquid. "Why are you amazed that I know the rules? I read that lease very carefully."

Maggie merely held her mug, knowing it would be at least five minutes before the coffee cooled enough for her taste. "Then you know that I have two more months before it expires. If I wanted to move before then—which

I assure you I don't—I'd either have to sublet or pay the whole amount due, because I've entered into a valid contract to live here till the end of June.''

''That's the way leases work,'' he agreed.

''Exactly. It's a legal contract, and as long as I have a lease, it's exactly as if I own this section of the house. So what makes you think you can just send me a letter and make me move?''

''Clause seven, paragraph two,'' he said succinctly. ''Equivalent housing.''

Maggie laughed. ''You call what you're offering equal to this?''

Karr looked around once more. The silence stretched painfully till almost a minute had gone by. Then he shrugged and looked directly at Maggie. ''Nope,'' he said easily.

She hadn't expected him to agree with her, and the hairs at the back of her neck warned that something wasn't right. Perhaps he'd admitted it only because they were alone, so she couldn't prove a thing—it would be her word against his. Nevertheless, he *had* conceded the point.

She pressed her advantage. ''Well, that leaves us—''

He interrupted. ''What I'm offering is a whole lot better.''

Maggie gave a genteel little snort. ''Says who?''

''Let's do a little comparing. You get your choice between a three-bedroom town house with a garden and a garage, or a condo with a fireplace and a hot tub, or an apartment with a clubhouse, pool and fully equipped gym right on the site, for the same amount of money you're paying now.''

''But only for the remaining two months of my lease.''

He shrugged. ''Those are the breaks. It's still a good deal, even for just two months. Do you know what those units rent for normally?''

"A whole lot more than Eagle's Landing," Maggie said dryly.

"True—but you get what you pay for. What do you do, anyway?"

"I'm the associate editor of a magazine."

"Oh, that's right, my secretary told me. The editor, hmm? Then I doubt you'd have too much trouble affording the rent, even at my supposedly outlandish prices. Or are you just too cheap to pay the going rate?"

Maggie snapped, "My finances are none of your affair!"

He looked a little surprised at her vehemence, and Maggie swallowed hard. She didn't have to explain to anyone how her budget had gotten in such a mess—but she'd only cause increased curiosity if she let it be known how sensitive a subject money was.

"I wasn't asking for a financial statement," he said mildly. "I still think you'd have trouble making a case that giving up a one-room apartment on the third floor of a shabby old house is any great sacrifice, no matter how much money's involved."

"It isn't simply a matter of money, anyway," Maggie argued. "How about the aesthetic value of this apartment? It's like living in a treehouse, which is a whole lot different than the average condo. You may not have any appreciation of charm or beauty, Mr. Elliot, but—"

"Oh, I wouldn't go that far," Karr drawled. His gaze was resting appreciatively on her face, and the sparkle in his eyes had grown even more wicked.

Maggie gritted her teeth. "I know, you find it in women," she snapped, "not old buildings. Spare me the sexist views, please—I'm not interested."

"Since when is it sexist for a man to find a woman attractive?" he said softly, and leaned forward as if to touch her.

Tripp raised his head and growled a little, and Karr withdrew his hand. "Have you considered oiling that dog?" he inquired. "He sounds as if he's rusty. So which development would you prefer? I'd take you around myself and show you the available units—"

"How thoughtful of you," Maggie murmured.

"Isn't it? The other tenants didn't get such personal service. But you see, I'm afraid I can't. I've got plans for the evening, and—" He glanced at his wristwatch. "I'm late already. Perhaps tomorrow?"

"I'll be busy tomorrow."

He set his mug on the tray and stood up. "Better not let it wait too long," he warned. "The town houses in particular are going fast."

"I'm not interested in a town house."

"Well, that might be a good choice, as the lawn would be a nuisance to keep up when you aren't used to it. And I must say I think the hot tubs make the condos very appealing."

"The last thing on earth I want is a condo."

"Really? Well, everyone to his own taste, I suppose. Not that the apartments aren't nice. That's where most of your neighbors decided to move, and of course they're the least expensive, but—"

Maggie gritted her teeth. "I have a lease, and I'm not leaving here."

Karr smiled. "Yes, you are. Your thirty days are up next Wednesday. And since today's Thursday..."

"But I haven't had thirty days," Maggie said stubbornly. "I only got the official notice today."

"It's not my fault you don't read your mail."

"I wasn't even here—I've been traveling for nearly a month."

"After such a long vacation, no wonder you're concerned about paying the rent. But that's beside the point. The letter was delivered in plenty of time, and according to the lease—'' His voice held a note of feigned concern. "You *have* read your lease? Fine print and all?"

"Of course I have." Not lately, Maggie admitted, but she certainly wasn't going to confess the fact to him. The minute he was out the door she'd find it, that was sure.

"According to the lease, sending notice of changes by ordinary first-class mail is considered sufficient. And this is a simple change in the lease, really—nothing complex at all."

"You call being evicted a simple change in the lease?"

"You're not being evicted," Karr pointed out. "Yet."

Maggie bounded to her feet and dug her fists into her hips. "Is that a threat? I suppose if I'm still here next Thursday morning you're going to send a SWAT team to blast me out!"

"Oh, I wouldn't like to say what I might do." His voice was gentle, but there was a steel thread underneath.

"Because you're not absolutely sure you're in the right, is that it? I think you're afraid a judge would agree that I haven't had adequate time to react to this—this incredible infringement on my rights."

"Do you, now?" He sounded almost admiring.

For a moment Maggie was sure she'd struck a nerve. Now they were getting somewhere!

"Personally, I can't see that your long trip is my problem," he went on. "Where were you, anyway? Lounging on a beach on a desert island? That's a nice tan you've got."

He'd certainly looked her over closely enough to know, Maggie thought irritably. "I was working."

A note of envy crept into his voice. "A thirty-day business trip that obviously involved a lot of sun... That's some job."

"It's no crime to fit in some time on the beach between interviews," Maggie said crisply. "There are certain advantages to my job, but it's still a pressure cooker of a position, and the last thing I need is to come home to this kind of trouble!''

"That," Karr said, "is hardly my problem. But you think it over, and we'll talk about it tomorrow.''

He was almost to the door when Maggie found her voice. "As long as you're treating me like the little woman," she called, "there's one line you've missed. Aren't you going to tell me I'm cute when I'm mad?''

"Oh, no," Karr said calmly. "I wouldn't want to be the one responsible for you getting a big head over a compliment like that.''

Maggie read clause seven, paragraph two for the sixth time, and in a fit of pique she crumpled the lease into a ball and flung it into the fireplace. Why had she been so blind when she signed the thing, not to see that there wasn't a single tiny loophole for a tenant who wanted to break the lease, but there was a glaring one for the landlord?

Oh, be realistic, she reminded herself. The truth was, she'd been so taken with Eagle's Landing on her first visit—and so desperate for an affordable place to live— that she'd probably have signed a contract that was a great deal more restrictive.

She had paid no attention to the clause because the idea of breaking her lease had never occurred to her. Even after her debts were repaid and she could afford a higher rent, she couldn't imagine leaving her treehouse of her own free will.

But the fact was, her debts weren't repaid—and they wouldn't be for another two years, at least—and in the meantime she couldn't afford a higher rent. Which left her with a problem.

If she'd had proper notification, she could have sought out another inexpensive place to live. Thirty days would have been little enough time as it was, but she probably could have managed. To find something affordable in less than a week would be impossible. The alternative—to take up Karr Elliot's offer for two short months and then move again—would be crazy. Her job didn't allow time for foolishness like that. She was facing a major deadline as it was. In fact, she ought to be working tonight, instead of fretting about living arrangements.

What made it particularly painful was that this was the second time she was losing what had seemed to be a permanent refuge.

She walked over to the window. It was dark now, and the moon was just rising above the trees, bathing Eagle's Landing in its silvery glow. From any angle she could look out into the tops of the oaks and maples. The ancient oak on the west side of the house was so tall and so broad that at night she could lie in bed and listen to the rhythmic scrape of its branches against the brick and slate. It always seemed to whisper reassurance—telling her that she wasn't alone.

Which was silly, of course. She liked being alone. As a child, and even as a young adult, she'd never had space and silence—and she'd wanted it desperately. That longing for solitude was a good deal of what had gotten her into the mess she was in now.

Buying a condominium had looked like such a good deal, after years spent living in boxy, noisy apartments shared with multiple roommates. Maggie had been on the job as an editorial assistant at *Today's Woman* for a year, her bank account was growing slowly but solidly, and her future was bright. There was already the possibility of a promotion, and someday she would be able to afford a place of her very own.

Then Darien Parker had come along. She'd met him at a party and dated him casually for a month before—over dinner one night, after she'd told him how tired she was of roommates—he'd shown her that someday was closer than she'd ever dreamed.

He had an inside track with a developer he knew, he said, and he could get her a deal on a brand-new condo. It was so new, in fact, that she could watch it be finished, and decide herself what color the carpet should be and whether she wanted natural wood or high-fashion gloss for her kitchen cabinets. To Maggie, who had never been able to paint a wall without getting approval from a landlord, it was heaven just to think about the options.

Her own place. Her own four walls...

If, that was, she could just come up with a down payment. A small one would do, Darien told her, because he would vouch for her with his friend—but of course, the more she could pay in advance, the less her monthly mortgage would be. He'd shown her how, with all the extra benefits of home ownership figured in, the condo would end up costing her less each month than the rent on an apartment. It was a deal so good that it would be insane to turn it down.

So Maggie closed her savings account, took the maximum advance on her credit cards, borrowed against her car and cashed in her tiny pension plan. The amount of money she could get her hands on was astounding, she'd thought proudly—not bad for a kid from the slums who'd only managed college by waiting tables and studying through the night till her eyes were always bloodshot, to keep her grades high enough to qualify for scholarship help.

She'd signed the papers, and the check, with shaking hands, and then she went to walk through the unfinished condo and dream of the home it would one day be. Maybe it would even be a home for two, she'd thought, for though it was too soon to make any firm decisions about their future, she and Darien were spending a great deal of time together.../.

Six weeks later, the developer was arrested and charged with fraud. It was no consolation that he was still in prison somewhere, because for all Maggie knew, her condo was sitting there yet without a roof, its plywood subfloor sagging under winter snows, its half-framed walls warped by wind and rain.

She couldn't even sell the shell, for it didn't belong to her after all, the investigators had told her gently. The project had been a scam from the start, and every one of the condos had been sold to at least three buyers.

Maggie's money—every single asset she'd been able to scrape together in the world—was gone, with nothing to show for it. She'd lost her car, and she was still paying back the other loans.

But even that hadn't been the worst of it. The cruelest blow had come when she called Darien, frantic—almost hysterical—in the hope that he could fix things, and he'd told her with a sneer that she'd been the easiest mark of them all. All he'd had to do was take her out, he'd said, and she'd been putty in his hands....

Maggie had cried for a week, and then had lifted her chin and made up her mind that she would not be defeated. She had pulled herself up from the slum. She could rise above this. But she would never be such a fool again. She would rely only on herself.

Once she'd had the promise of her own space, she found she couldn't bear to go on sharing an apartment with others, and that was when she'd found Eagle's Landing. It had been more than a place to live—it was a haven, a sanctuary. There was nothing like it. No matter how long she looked, she'd never find anything that could compare to her treehouse.

She couldn't have it, of course. Sooner or later, she would have to go. But it wasn't fair for Karr Elliot to rob her of her home without even giving her breathing space—the rest of her lease, or at least the same amount of notice that everyone else at Eagle's Landing had gotten.

Somewhere, she told herself, there must be a judge who'd agree.

She reached into the side pocket of her briefcase for her notebook calendar and paged through it till she found the unlisted home phone number of the magazine's legal counsel. She didn't know Chad Buckley well, but surely if she told him how important this was, and how pressured she was for time, he wouldn't mind being disturbed at home.

She recognized his voice, and hesitated, for it sounded as if there was a party going on. She could hear the clink of glasses and the murmur of voices and laughter. "Chad? it's Margaret Rawlings from *Today's Woman*."

His voice warmed. "Well, hello, Margaret." He pronounced all three syllables, as if he was caressing the name.

Maggie frowned. That didn't sound like the businesslike Chad Buckley she'd encountered at occasional staff meetings.

"There's nothing wrong at the magazine, I hope?" he went on.

"No—I'm afraid this is personal business. I'm sorry to call you at home, but I'm in a jam."

"What can I do for you?"

"I'm having a problem with my lease, and I wanted to ask your advice. I know how busy you are, but perhaps I could buy you lunch tomorrow?"

"I assume this is a matter that needs quick action?"

"Well, yes. I just found out—"

"Then why don't we take care of it tonight? It's early yet. Come over to my house and—"

"Aren't you having a party?"

"Oh, it's nobody important. I can get rid of them by the time you arrive."

Definitely not the Chad Buckley she was used to, Maggie thought dryly. "That's very thoughtful, but I think lunch would be a better idea."

"Well, if you insist on worrying about it overnight, I guess that's your right. I'll give you a call at the magazine in the morning, shall I?"

Maggie put the telephone down with mixed feelings. With a plan of action under way, she could relax a little. On the other hand, if she'd had any inkling that Chad Buckley had something besides magazine law on his mind when he looked at her...

She'd probably have called him anyway, she concluded, since he was the only attorney listed in her little black book.

She was rummaging in the kitchen for a snack when Libby tapped on the door a little later. "Honey? Are you feeling better?"

"I wasn't feeling bad, exactly."

"Well, I heard you shouting at someone."

"Oh—that was just Elliot the hotshot home wrecker. Want a cup of tea?"

Libby nodded and pulled up a chair. "What did he tell you?"

"Typical propaganda—how I'd better make up my mind right away because the town houses are going fast. You know the sort of stuff salesmen always say."

Libby looked doubtful.

Maggie surveyed the contents of the refrigerator with distaste. "I knew I should have stopped at the supermarket before I came home." She dug a loaf of bread out of the freezer and dropped two slices into the toaster. "Cheer up, Libby. It'll work out somehow. Aren't you going to ask about my trip? I've got so much material for this special edition that I'm going to ask Brian tomorrow for another sixteen pages. And if he doesn't give it to me—"

There was another knock at the half-open door, and Dan Montgomery put his head in. "I thought I'd find you up here," he told his wife. "Have the two of you solved the problem yet?"

Maggie shrugged. "Not exactly, but I'm going to talk to a lawyer tomorrow. We'll see what he can do."

"I hope he hurries." Libby kissed her husband's cheek. "If the town houses are going fast—"

Maggie looked at her in astonishment. "Oh, Libby, of course they're not! Elliot the Great was just saying that to make us scared that we'd lose out."

"Well, he succeeded with me," Libby said stubbornly.

"I'm still having trouble with the whole idea. Nobody ever told me that Eagle's Landing was for sale." Maggie's toast popped up and she carefully spread the slices with strawberry jam, cut them into halves and offered the plate to the Montgomerys. Dan bit into a piece.

Libby shook her head. "I hadn't heard it, either, so don't look at me. Maybe it was the reverse—Elliot wanted it badly enough to seek out the owners and make an offer."

"But why?" Dan asked. "It's not exactly a financial winner for the landlord. The heating bill alone must be immense." He took a second chunk of toast. "Elliot said something about upscale housing, but—"

"The place was elegant once," Maggie mused. "And it could be again. If it was completely renovated and made into five or six apartments instead of a dozen, they'd command a premium price." She put two more slices of bread in the toaster.

"Maybe," Libby said doubtfully, and looked at Dan. "I think we'd better take care of this tomorrow, don't you?"

"Take care of what?" Maggie asked suspiciously.

"We've been talking it over," Dan said. "And we're going to go ahead. Take the town house, I mean, and hope we can buy it in a few months."

"Traitors," Maggie said matter-of-factly.

"We were only waiting till we'd talked to you," Libby pointed out. "But there's no point in holding out. And if there's a shortage—"

"What can I do to convince you there isn't? It's a ploy, Libby, and you fell for it."

"Still," Dan said, "I think we'd better not wait too long. We've got to do something, and this seems the best alternative. If we're really careful with the budget, we can end up owning a place of our own."

"I'm going to get a job, too," Libby said. "We've gotten along fine here with me not working, but I can't let Dan carry all the weight."

Maggie finished off the last bit of toast. "I can't argue with you," she said finally. "We all have to make our own decisions."

Libby reached across the table to touch Maggie's arm. "Come with me tomorrow and look at the town houses," she urged. "Maybe you'll be surprised, and we can be next-door neighbors this time."

If it was going to take three jobs between the two of them for the Montgomerys to afford a town house, how did Libby think Maggie could swing it?

Maggie laughed a little hollowly. "Doubtful. From what Elliot the Great said, there probably aren't two units left, much less ones that are next to each other!"

In the conference room atop the Metro Tower on Chicago's Magnificent Mile, the regular meeting of the editorial board was breaking up. Maggie gathered her stack of folders and followed the editor-in-chief to his office. "Brian," she said, "I really need sixteen more pages in the anniversary issue. I've got so much incredible stuff you won't believe it."

"Maggie," he said, without turning around. "I've explained this once already. We've pushed the budget to the limit, and there's no more space to be had."

"I'll bet if I called the owners and asked them to increase the budget—"

He wheeled to face her. "You wouldn't do that, Rawlings!"

"Of course not," Maggie said calmly. "For one thing, it would be professional suicide to go over your head. But *you* could call them." She saw a glimmer of uncertainty in his face and pushed her advantage. "Brian, you know this is going to be a great issue. But it could be even better with a little more space."

"Sixteen pages more? Maggie—"

"How about a compromise? I'll take twelve additional pages for editorial, and advertising gets four more to sell."

"How about you get back to work?"

Maggie leaned against the jamb of his office door and smiled.

Brian rubbed a hand over his brow. "I'll try for eight," he offered.

"Try for sixteen and settle for eight," Maggie recommended. "That's what I always do." She ignored his bellow and crossed to her office, one of a group of tiny, glass-walled cubicles arranged in a half-circle around a computer station where a single editorial assistant sat, juggling the needs of half a dozen associate editors.

And people think the magazine business is glamorous, Maggie thought. The public image of a powerful editor included a big office with a walnut desk and a private secretary. She smiled at her daydream.

"Chad Buckley wants you to meet him for lunch at Coq au Vin in twenty minutes," the editorial assistant said. "What have you been doing now, Maggie, that you're in legal trouble?"

"Who said I was, Carol?" She took the pink message slip the young woman held out.

"Because nobody would voluntarily have lunch with that lecher."

So Carol had no illusions about Chad. That was interesting, Maggie thought. "I hadn't noticed him chasing secretaries around desks," she said mildly.

Carol didn't bother to answer. Instead she murmured, "From the wrinkles on your forehead, you must be facing a libel suit, at least. Perhaps I should warn Brian—maybe he'll reward me with a promotion."

"To fiction editor, no doubt," Maggie said sweetly. "You're highly qualified for the position."

Carol grinned. "Will you write me a recommendation?"

"Of course, if it'll keep you from going after *my* job." Maggie dropped her folders on her desk and picked up the sage green jacket that matched her suede skirt.

Coq au Vin was one of the city's premier restaurants, always rated top on the list of five-star establishments, and it was seldom Maggie's choice for lunch unless she was on an expense account. But then, an hour in Chad Buckley's office would no doubt cost a lot more, she reflected philosophically as she gave her name to the maître d'.

"I'm joining Mr. Buckley," she added, and he bowed and almost clicked his heels as he led her to a secluded corner table.

Chad Buckley was already sipping sherry. He rose to hold her chair and snapped his fingers at a waiter. "Would you like sherry, Margaret, or something else?"

"Just iced tea, thanks."

"Very sensible. Let's take care of the business right away, shall we, so you can enjoy your lunch?"

Maggie handed him her lease and told him about her encounter with Karr Elliot. Chad made no comment. He pulled a pair of reading glasses out of his breast pocket and buried himself in the fine print of the lease, looking up only to order a grilled chicken salad.

Maggie toyed with her iced tea and watched him. Finally Chad pushed the lease across the table to her and folded his glasses. "It's a very clear-cut situation," he said. "As far as equivalent housing goes, I don't see that there's anything you can do. The intent of clause seven is very clear, and *equivalent* doesn't mean *the same*, Margaret—not in legal terms. You shouldn't have signed the lease, of course, but that's not much comfort now."

"All right. I guess I can't fight that one. But I haven't had proper notice. I certainly can't move by Wednesday."

"Well..." Chad looked at the lease again. "We can try. It's likely to be a delaying action, though, rather than a winning campaign."

"I know that's the best I can hope for. Will you fight it for me? I don't have much of a budget for legal work, but—"

"Of course I'll do my best. And you mustn't worry about the budget. I wouldn't dream of charging you."

Maggie sat up a little straighter. "That's very generous, Chad, but—"

He smiled. "You know, I had you all wrong, Margaret. The first time we met, you were so chilly I thought you weren't interested, so I never followed up, even though I really wanted to get to know you better. But now that you've found this excuse to call me—" He reached out to pat her hand. "I'm so glad, my dear."

And that, Maggie thought, was just one more annoyance to ring up to Karr Elliot's account!

CHAPTER THREE

MAGGIE was still steaming when she got back to her office. Elliot the Great was a menace, she fumed. The man didn't even have to be within twenty miles of her to mess up her life and make her normal protective instincts blow up like antique dynamite.

She stuffed the piled-high contents of her in basket into her briefcase and left a message on the computer system for anyone who might be looking for her that she'd be working at home for the foreseeable future.

"Or at least the next five days," she muttered. "While I still *have* a home."

She couldn't put any great faith in Chad Buckley as long as he thought her plea for help was only an excuse to get closer to him. And if he was right about her lease, approaching another attorney would end up accomplishing little and costing her money she couldn't afford.

I'll think about it later, she decided.

She spent her hour on the commuter train reading freelance articles sent in by hopeful writers, and by the time the train stopped at Eagleton she'd made a decent dent in the pile. One never knew when there might be a rare jewel hidden in the slush—but it didn't look as if today was one of those lucky days.

She stopped at the post office to return the articles she couldn't use, and with her bag considerably lightened she caught the local bus. The ride was too jerky to do any serious work, but fortunately it was only a mile out to Eagle's Landing. Public transportation was a nuisance. She looked forward to having a car again once she was out from under her load of debt and could afford the payments and insurance.

With this new twist, however, that day would no doubt be postponed even longer. Maggie sighed. Of course, if she ended up back in the city, she wouldn't need or want a car....

Damn Karr Elliot, anyway. Why had he had to come along and mess up what had been a perfectly well-organized, sane and reasonable life?

When she got off the bus at the end of the long drive, there was no sign of human life, just the random, careless songs of a half-dozen birds and the irritable chatter of a squirrel annoyed by her presence. Maggie paused to talk to him for a moment, and he stared beadily at her before darting around the tree trunk and off into the woods.

Everything else was quiet. But then Eagle's Landing usually was quiet. The house had been built for silence, with thick walls and floors. Dan and Libby and Maggie were by far the youngest of the residents, and the wildest party Maggie could remember in her three years in the house was a Sunday afternoon when Mr. Kelly, in one of the ground-floor apartments, had doled out his homemade dandelion wine by the thimbleful to all his fellow tenants.

The intense quiet was one of the big attractions of the place, as far as Maggie was concerned. When she was working on a special project, it was so much easier to concentrate in her quiet treehouse than in the bustle of the office. The memory of trying to do serious work in an ordinary apartment complex made her head ache.

It was midafternoon, and the sun was pleasantly warm on her shoulders as she walked up the long drive. The soft breeze caressed her face, whispering the promise of spring.

She paused once to shift her load to the other shoulder. Despite all the weight she'd dropped off at the post office, the briefcase was getting heavier with every step.

She heard the crunch of gravel and glanced over her shoulder as a black Mercedes purred up the drive and slowed to an idle beside her. But she didn't stop walking. There was no doubt in her mind who was at the wheel. None of the tenants had the kind of cash it took to drive a vehicle like that.

The passenger window lowered, and Karr leaned across the seat. "Hi." His voice seemed huskier than ever. "I thought you said you were busy today."

"I was," Maggie said. "In fact, I still am." She tapped the side of the leather briefcase.

The car crept along beside her for another ten feet. "Would you like a lift to the house?"

She shrugged. "Might as well. Thanks."

Karr's eyebrows lifted. "A bit grudging, but it'll do."

"Sorry. I didn't mean to sound ungrateful."

Compared to the hard bench on the commuter train, the Merecedes's leather seat was sheer luxury, and the lulling motion of the car was so unlike the rocking of the local bus that she felt as if she was hardly moving at all.

"You know," Karr said thoughtfully, "my town house development is only three blocks from the train station."

"Really?" Maggie kept her voice cool so he couldn't possibly mistake politeness for enthusiasm.

"That's not much longer than this driveway. But I forgot—you have no interest in gardening, so the town houses are out. Well, the condos are right on the city transit system. Step off the bus and you're practically at the front door."

"That's hardly a recommendation, in my book."

"I'll bet this is a cold, uncomfortable walk in the winter," he speculated. "But then you won't have to worry about it any more, will you? By the time winter comes again, you'll be gone."

"That's eight or nine months," Maggie mused. "All right, that offer seems fair. I'll stay till the end of November, and when the cold sets in—"

"*Long* gone," Karr said firmly.

She looked at him innocently. "You mean that wasn't an offer?"

"You know, I had you pegged as the sort who would want everything cut, dried and signed on the dotted line, with an engagement calendar set up six months ahead—"

"Well, in the magazine business—"

"And an annual budget figured to the penny."

That was uncomfortably close to the truth, and Maggie didn't care to admit it. "Well, don't you like to know what you're going to be doing well ahead of time?"

"Only where my business is concerned. Which is why you're moving next week." The Mercedes pulled up in the small paved lot behind the house.

Maggie shook her head. "No, that's why I'm *not* moving next week. I want time to consider and make a reasonable decision—time your so-called notice didn't let me have. Thanks for the ride." She couldn't help sighing just a little as she picked up her briefcase.

Karr didn't miss her reaction, of course. "Aren't you looking forward to those two very long flights of stairs?" He came around the car to open the door for her. "My apartment complex has an elevator."

"What a novel idea," Maggie murmured. "Did you think of it all by yourself?"

"Would you like me to carry that bag upstairs for you?"

She tipped her head to one side and studied his face. He looked innocent, but she knew better. "Now that's a loaded question," she mused. "If I say yes, you can point out that it would be much easier to carry if I lived anywhere but here. And if I say no—"

He was smiling. "The question wasn't as loaded as that bag obviously is. Give it here." He reached for the strap of her briefcase. His hand brushed her shoulder, and despite the weight of her tweed jacket Maggie could sense the roughness of his work-hardened palm against her skin.

Now that's silly, she told herself. She started to glance at him, wondering if he'd felt her suppressed shiver, and then turned quickly away, not sure if she wanted to know what he was thinking.

She spotted a colorful brochure in the back of the Mercedes and reached for it. The cover showed a long row of identical town houses. The only distinguishing feature was the various colors the front doors were painted. But even all of those harmonized, as if the shades had been chosen from a narrow palette. "Do you have an extra copy of this?" she asked.

"A whole trunkful. Take as many as you like."

"One will do." She opened the pamphlet studiously. Let him think she was interested, after all, she decided. If he thought she was about to surrender, he might slow down any action he'd been considering.

"The floor plans are on the back," he said. "Your friends the Montgomerys seemed to like the layout of the Wakefield unit best."

"That's nice." Maggie tucked the pamphlet into the pocket of her jacket. So Libby and Dan had followed through. Well, she wasn't surprised, and she also wasn't about to let Karr Elliot see that she was disappointed.

"I expect they'll be moving over the weekend." Karr held the side door for her, and Maggie stepped into the downstairs hallway.

It was flooded with light. The pocket doors that led into the drawing rooms were open, and sunshine poured through the library windows. The rooms were empty, but there were dust balls here and there, dents in the carpet where furniture had stood and darker patches on the wallpaper where pictures had once hung. Still, despite the worn appearance of the rooms, Maggie had no trouble recognizing the potential Karr must have seen as well—the high ceilings, ornate carved woodwork and leaded glass that were simply unavailable in modern buildings. Instead of a dozen small, dark and rather dingy apartments, there could be half as many light, airy and luxurious ones. It was space that would command a premium price, Maggie knew.

"You know," she said thoughtfully, "as long as we're talking about elevators... Unless you put one in, that attic space I've got will be practically useless. Nobody's going to pay big money for a third-floor walkup. So—"

"So why don't I just let you stay, and pay your pittance of a rent? Nice try, Maggie, my dear."

She shrugged. "It will take years' worth of rent to pay for an elevator."

"I'm touched that you're watching out for my bottom line." He started up the stairs. Maggie followed more slowly, looking over the banister at the empty, lonely rooms on the ground floor.

This morning when she'd left the house it had been easy to pretend that the silence was normal, that Mr. Kelly was simply sleeping a little later than usual and Mrs. Harper was still sitting over her breakfast and her newspaper. But seeing the rooms open for the first time, Maggie was forced to admit that half the residents were already gone, and the other half would soon move on, as well.

Karr seemed to read her mind. "By the beginning of next week it'll be pretty lonely around here."

Only if you stay away, she thought, and frowned. She'd meant that the other way around, of course—that she'd be happier if he *did* leave her in peace. "Oh, I'm never lonely. I'm far too busy."

"I know. That unusual job of yours must be one long adventure."

"It certainly is." She squared her shoulders and hurried to catch up with him on the landing. "Just now I'm putting together a special section to celebrate the tenth anniversary of *Today's Woman.*"

"Celebrating the accomplishments of the last decade?"

She tried to find irony in his tone, because she was sure it must be there, but she couldn't. "Of course there's some of that, but the theme of the issue is looking forward to the next decade—to tomorrow's woman and beyond."

"Making a better world for your daughters?"

Maggie shrugged. "I doubt I'll ever get around to having any. My point is, the special section is why I was gone so long on this trip. And now that I'm back, I'm under a really rigid deadline to get it put together. It's the biggest feature section the magazine's ever done. So you see, I'm not being unreasonable to want more time. I can't possibly move and do my work, too."

"Oh, I don't know. Send a crew of guys upstairs and they could have you out of here in a couple of hours."

She stopped on the landing. "Is that a threat?"

"Only if you want to take it that way. I meant it as a simple statement of fact—you don't have that much stuff."

"I have more than it looks like. But I'd have to sort and pack it myself, or I'd never find anything again."

"In the town house, you could have a whole floor to spread things out and sort. And an office with a door, too—so you could close it off and forget about your job."

"I don't want to forget my job, thank you. I like it quite well. And I have a perfectly adequate work space right here."

They reached the top of the last flight, and behind the locked door of the apartment, Tripp started to bark a greeting. His eager yips were interspersed with low growls, though, and Maggie turned to her unwelcome guest. "You know, I'm beginning to think Tripp doesn't like you," she said solicitously. "Perhaps you'd better not come in."

"Tripp? Is that the toupee's name?"

"He has a very aristocratic name that he won't answer to. He's been Tripp since he was a puppy because he was always under my feet."

"The size he is, it would be hard for him to be any-where else," Karr said unsympathetically. "Didn't the landlords get complaints about him growling at the other tenants? Or did they think he was just a mechanical toy?"

"He only growls at people who upset him," Maggie said with a smile. She took her briefcase. "Thanks for carrying this. Now I really do need to get to work."

"Of course. So do I."

Maggie's curiosity overcame her. "Exactly what are you planning to do to the house that can't wait a few more weeks?"

His eyebrows rose slightly. "Oh, I wouldn't want to keep you from your very important work with dull explanations."

"Have you considered starting on the ground floor," she suggested, "and working your way up?"

He tipped his head to one side. "And by the time I get all the way to the attic, you'll be out? I'll give it some thought."

Inside the apartment, the telephone started to ring, and Maggie fumbled for her key.

Karr said, "I'll be in touch, all right?"

He made it sound as if they were casual friends parting after a chance meeting, Maggie thought irritably, and exchanging hypocritical promises about vague future plans. Too bad she wouldn't be getting off that easily.

She stepped over Tripp to set her briefcase carefully on the library table, then reached for the telephone.

"How'd your lunch go?" her editorial assistant asked.

"Don't ask, Carol." Maggie pulled her computer out of the case and began sorting manuscripts into stacks.

"It was that enjoyable, hm? Brian said to tell you he got the extra eight pages you wanted—and you'd better make them look as sharp as anything this magazine's ever published, because it's not his neck on the line now, it's yours. That's a direct quote."

"I assumed it was," Maggie said dryly.

The instant she hung up, Tripp planted himself in front of her and gave one short, emphatic bark.

"Not now, darling," Maggie told him. "I simply haven't time to take you for a walk this minute."

But she'd forgotten two things—how stubborn Tripp could be, and that Libby had probably spoiled him rotten in the last month, jumping up to take him out whenever he wanted. Maggie cast a guilty look at her computer and went to get his leash.

She heard voices in the front drawing room and saw the silhouettes of two men bent over a roll of paper spread on the window seat at the front of the room.

Tripp growled very softly.

"Yes, I know, it's Elliot the Great and you don't like him," Maggie muttered, "but mind your manners anyway. He's not on your territory now, you're on his."

Tripp ignored her and unleashed a peal of barks. Karr crossed the room to the pocket doors and leaned against the jamb. "Well, well, if it isn't Maggie. I'm glad to see you cracking right down to that important work of yours."

Maggie gritted her teeth. "Don't you dare tell me that if I lived in your condos, it wouldn't be so hard to let the dog out."

"It's true. For a while, anyway, until he growled at the wrong neighbor and ended up on a barbecue grill." Karr turned back to his companion and pointed at the roll of paper. "That's got to be taken down first, and then that one. But as for the rest, I think we'd better wait and see."

See what? Maggie was dying to ask, or better yet to sneak a look at that drawing. She suspected it was a blueprint of the house. What did Karr think had to go? Surely he wasn't talking about walls. But it was almost as bad if he intended to tear out the wonderful ornamentation—

He might be, though, she realized. All he'd ever said was something about upscale housing, but he'd never specified what his definition included.

She looked up at the frieze that decorated the hallway, yards and yards of carved wood depicting grapevines and heavy bunches of ripe fruit. She'd looked at it often, and admired it as a good example of its type, even though the subject didn't exactly move her. But she'd never seen it this way, with sunlight and shadow playing tag through the vines and around the grapes. This was how it had been intended to look, and it would be a sin to tear it down.

It wasn't any of her business, she reminded herself. But it was immensely frustrating not to know what Karr was planning to do with this house.

Libby knocked on Maggie's door a couple of hours later and quietly put her head in. "I'm sorry to bother you," she said when Maggie looked up from the screen of her laptop computer. "But Dan and I wondered if you'd like to join us for a celebration dinner tonight."

"Celebrating your falling in love with the...what was it? Wakefield model?"

"Not exactly," Libby said carefully.

Maggie's eyes widened. "Elliot got it wrong?"

"Oh, no. It's the Wakefield we liked best. But it's the most wonderful thing, Maggie."

Maggie thoughtfully saved the computer file she was working on and pushed her chair back. She hadn't seen Libby this excited in a year.

"We were sitting there in the office with the rental agent, and at the last minute, with the lease right in front of us, I got cold feet and my fingers just wouldn't work. I asked Dan what we were going to do if we couldn't scrape up the down payment by Christmas so we could buy, and I said maybe we'd be better off to take these last few days and look for something else, something we could afford no matter what."

Maggie's jaw dropped in astonishment. "Libby, I had no idea you were such a tremendous negotiator. That was a stroke of genius!" And one in the eye for Karr Elliot, which didn't hurt her feelings, either.

"That's just it—I wasn't trying. It simply happened."

"Not that it matters. So you're staying here? That's wonderful. With both of us fighting, maybe we can even make the case that—"

"Oh, no, dear. We're moving on Monday. You see, the agent excused herself to let us talk about it privately, and a few minutes later Karr came in."

The agent recognized a major-league problem and called in the top pitcher, Maggie thought with foreboding. And now Libby was on first-name terms with Elliot the Great.

"And..." Libby started to grin. "Well, the upshot is that we're not just renting the town house, we're buying it. Now isn't that something to celebrate?"

"Depends," Maggie said dryly. "How did he talk you into this? Last night you couldn't afford it."

"He didn't talk us into anything, Maggie. I wish you wouldn't be so paranoid about Karr, he's really a dear. He just said he wished he'd known we were thinking of buying, because there were all sorts of financing possibilities that no one would have mentioned since they thought we were only interested in renting, and when he started explaining what he could do..."

"In other words, he cut you a special deal to get you out of here."

Libby considered that and shrugged. "I suppose he did. But I can't say that I care, Maggie. We signed the papers right there, and we went straight back to the house and walked through and stopped in every room to hug and laugh."

It all sounded so horribly familiar that Maggie's mouth went dry with fear.

It's not the same, she told herself. Karr might be playing games with financing, but at least there *was* a town house, finished and ready to move into. And the Montgomerys would be the only ones to claim it.

"Oh, darling, it's ours," Libby said softly, "and it's so wonderful. Everything smells new and fresh, and the appliances have never been used, and the space—oh, Maggie, to have a real dining room! Well, it's not a *room*, actually, more like an alcove, but it's so much more than we have here!"

She was so happy that Maggie couldn't find it in her heart to do anything but smile and agree that without a doubt it had been the best thing ever to happen to Dan and Libby.

But under her relaxed surface, every muscle was clenched hard. That crack of Karr's about "your friends the Montgomerys" liking the Wakefield model best... Maggie hadn't given it a thought at the time, but in replaying the memory, she could hear the satisfaction in his tone. He hadn't been delighted that Libby and Dan had fallen in love with the town house, or because they'd bought it instead of renting. He'd been so almighty self-satisfied because he had been able to eliminate Maggie's only remaining source of moral support.

And what really ticked her off was that he'd done it so neatly she couldn't even get angry at Libby and Dan for falling into the trap.

On Sunday afternoon, the busybody in the second-floor back moved out. Maggie happened to be going out to the supermarket just as a couple of young men were roping down the last piece of furniture in the back of an Elliot Development Corporation truck, and she hesitated for a moment before going over to speak to the woman who was supervising the work.

Maggie had tried to be neighborly when the woman first moved in—she'd taken a casserole downstairs and introduced herself, but the woman had never been friendly. And even though she'd spent all her time spying on the other tenants, Maggie would have been sorry to see her leave without even the chance to say goodbye.

The busybody sniffed when Maggie asked where she was moving, and looked around cautiously before she answered. "It's a little apartment in Mr. Elliot's complex," she said finally. "He said the rent won't ever be much more than here, but you can believe I'm going to keep my eyes open. He doesn't need to think he can pull something fishy on me."

How sad, Maggie thought, that a gesture which sounded so generous was received with such suspicion.

"I wish you all the best," she said, and only after the truck was gone did she realize that though she hadn't actually stood up for Karr, she had mentally jumped to his defense nonetheless.

Of course, from all appearances the woman's new apartment *was* a generous deal, to say nothing of the work of actually moving her into it. And the busybody had been a paranoid sort from the moment she'd moved in; it wasn't difficult to discount her opinions. Still, for Maggie to suddenly find herself supporting Karr Elliot's behavior came as a bit of a shock.

She wheeled a cart through the supermarket aisles, trying to remember what was already on her cabinet shelves at home. Since Libby and Dan were in the depths of packing, with the movers scheduled to come early Monday morning, Maggie had invited them upstairs for a last dinner together.

Not that it was like the proverbial last meal, she thought. After all, they'd be only a few miles away—depending, of course, on where Maggie herself ended up. There would no doubt be many more evenings together. But it would be different, once they moved. They'd have new acquaintances, and so would she. Their lives would go in different directions...

"You may stop feeling sorry for yourself," she said firmly, and then realized she was standing in the frozen foods aisle holding a container of orange juice that she neither wanted nor needed, with a couple of interested spectators looking on. Maggie colored, put the orange juice back, and hurried on to the dairy section.

She was sitting on a bench in front of the store, munching a piece of licorice from a pack she'd just opened and waiting for the taxi she'd called to take her home, when a black Mercedes pulled up. Karr left the engine running and got out, pulling off a pair of aviator sunglasses as he came toward her.

"Hi," he said cheerfully. "Fancy meeting you here."

Maggie looked around. She could think of no reason for him to be in this particular shopping area in the middle of a Sunday afternoon. He didn't strike her as a gourmet cook—and if he was going into the store, he'd hardly have left the engine running. But there was nothing else in this strip mall but a dry cleaner's and a dentist's office, both of which were closed on weekends.

"Is it my imagination," she said dryly, "or do you have radar where I'm concerned?"

He smiled warmly. "You've noticed! Can I dare hope you feel it, too?"

"As a matter of fact, the way I feel when you're around can best be described as extremely uncomfortable."

"Are you certain that's me? It could just be a result of too much licorice." He put one foot up on the bench beside her, leaning an elbow casually on his knee. "I said I'd stay in touch, you know. It's been—my goodness, almost forty-eight hours since we've talked. I didn't want you to feel neglected."

"Well, now that you've made sure of that, feel free to go about your business." She looked around the mall once more. "What *is* your business here, anyway?"

"I came out to Eagle's Landing to see you, and Libby told me you were here. So I came to give you a ride home so you didn't have to juggle your grocery bags on the bus."

He really had a very nice smile, Maggie thought. His eyes lit up, and his teeth gleamed, and wonderful little laugh lines came to life everywhere. The whole picture teased at her senses, and she wished she hadn't noticed. It was going to be even more difficult to ignore him if every time he grinned at her she wanted to smile back.

"Thanks, but I've already called a taxi. And speaking of Libby, she and Dan signed the contract on the town house in an awful hurry. Aren't you just a little worried about whether their mortgage financing will go through?"

"Oh, it will."

"Spoken like a man who knows," Maggie murmured. "I didn't realize it was so easy to get a mortgage these days."

"Didn't you?" Karr asked easily. "Would you like one? I'll see what I can do." His tone was so casual he might have been offering an ice cream cone.

"No, thanks. I'm not particularly interested in the sort of creative financing deals that developers seem to specialize in."

He frowned a little. Just then Maggie's taxi pulled up, and she started to gather her bags. Instead of helping— as he would if he'd been a gentleman, Maggie thought irritably—Karr wandered over to the taxi.

She turned just in time to see him give something to the driver. The taxi took off, and Karr came back, dusting his hands.

"What—" she began.

"There's no point in him trailing out to Eagle's Landing when I've got nothing better to do this afternoon anyway. I'll swap you a ride for a piece of your licorice."

"I don't have much of a choice now, do I?"

He grinned and started loading her purchases into the back of the car, handling the three bags of food as easily as if they had no weight at all. "There's a lot of stuff here. Am I invited to the party?"

"Who said I'm having one? Maybe I'm just stocking up. I don't get to the store all that often."

He helped Maggie into the passenger seat. "Why don't you have a car, anyway?"

She shrugged. "Too much bother. I seldom have so much to carry that I can't take the bus, and I wouldn't drive into the city anyway—a car is purely a nuisance in the Loop. So why have it sitting around unused for weeks at a time?''

The glance he sent her way was quizzical. Maggie couldn't understand why. Her explanation was perfectly rational, even if it didn't happen to be quite the truth.

"This one's nice, though," she added generously.

"Thank you. If you like, I'll drive you past the condos and the town houses."

"Oh, that's all right. I wouldn't want to put you to any trouble."

"Don't give it a thought. Compared to all the trouble you've already been, this isn't even worth mentioning."

She glared at him, and realized that the corner of his mouth had curved very slightly upward. She gave up. Whatever she said was likely only to amuse him more, and she was obviously going to see the town houses and condos anyway.

As developments went, she had to admit they weren't bad. The town houses were lined up in a row, as the brochure had showed, with garages nestled between each unit, creating the illusion that each house stood alone. They weren't arranged in a straight line, however, but in a long, easy curve, so even though all the houses were as alike as peas in a pod, the effect was somehow gentler than the average town house complex.

Not that she approved, exactly, Maggie thought. And she wasn't about to tell him that the town houses were better than she'd expected. Karr would no doubt jump to the conclusion that she actually liked what she saw, and then she'd have no peace at all.

The condos were scattered over a hillside, and though the buildings were all alike, the varying placements meant that they didn't look like clones.

"Each building contains eight units," Karr said. "Four upstairs, four down. But we've designed the basic structure to place the units at angles, so a resident can look out from his front door and feel that his is the only home around."

"You know," Maggie mused, "I think I'd rather be shot at dawn than live in something called a *unit*."

He grinned, but he didn't answer.

"It's funny," Maggie mused, "but Libby didn't seem to think there was a shortage of town houses. If she had her pick of all the models—"

"I'd held back one of each, special, just for the Eagle's Landing people to look at. Libby got the last Wakefield."

"Oh, darn." Maggie's voice dripped irony.

"But I can't hold the remaining ones off the market any longer—I've got salespeople champing at the bit to get to work on that. Just as I've got people waiting impatiently for Wednesday, so they can start work at Eagle's Landing."

Maggie didn't bother to ask what sort of work. She knew she wouldn't get much of an answer. "What would you have done if I hadn't come back from my business trip before Wednesday?"

"I don't know. Probably waited a couple of weeks and then put your stuff in storage."

"Then there's really no reason you can't be patient a couple of weeks or so while I decide what to do, is there?"

"You've got till Wednesday," he said. There was nothing harsh about his voice, but there was an underlying strength that sent a chill rippling through Maggie's veins.

"That's utterly ridiculous," she said. Her resolution not to ask again about his plans collapsed. "What sort of work is so important that you can't wait a little while? Or start somewhere else and work around me?"

"Tell you what, my dear. After you've moved away from Eagle's Landing, I'll take you out for a cup of coffee and tell you all about it. And when it's all done, I'll give you the guided tour." The car pulled up beside the house, and he turned to face her. "You've got till dark on Wednesday."

"I'm not leaving, Karr."

He got out and set her bags onto the steps at the side of the house. "I don't know how I can be any more reasonable."

"You can leave me alone till Wednesday," Maggie muttered. "That would help."

"Yes, ma'am." But his tone was not nearly as servile as the words.

Maggie watched as the Mercedes vanished down the drive, feeling a little lost and empty. Perhaps that was just because Karr had made the deadline so specific; until now she'd been able to convince herself that there would be some flexibility, that eventually he would see the sense of her argument and give her the time she needed. She'd simply have to call Chad Buckley again and make sure he realized how important that delaying action was going to be.

Then Maggie squared her shoulders and looked at the three bags of food lined up neatly on the step. "That wasn't terribly bright of you," she mocked herself. "If you'd played your cards right, Elliot the Great would have helped carry the bags upstairs—and *then* you could have told him to get lost!"

CHAPTER FOUR

EAGLE'S Landing had always made noises. Creaks and rattles were part of the charm of an old house, Maggie had always thought, and she'd enjoyed getting to know the house's natural sounds. Mostly they were friendly ones—even companionable.

But on Monday, as the sun began to sink toward the west, Maggie found herself jumping at every noise. She told herself she was being silly, playing subconscious mind games simply because she knew she was alone. It really was stupid to be so sensitive about it. After all, she'd been the only one in the house on countless occasions before, and the fact had never bothered her.

But it was different knowing that this time no one else would be coming back to Eagle's Landing. In one of that long row of identical town houses, Dan and Libby were gleefully unpacking boxes or cooking their first dinner on the built-in barbecue grill in their brand-new kitchen. The other tenants were all settling into new places, as well. Only Maggie was left.

"And that's because you wanted to stay," she reminded herself.

Even Tripp seemed to sense a difference in the house. He'd abandoned his favorite position on the kitchen rug and was huddled at Maggie's feet instead, under the library table where she'd been working all afternoon. She'd been so involved in roughing out the main story for the special section that she hadn't even noticed when he'd moved. She'd just suddenly realized he was there, leaning against her ankles and practically shivering....

61

And no wonder. The apartment was chilly, and growing more so with each passing minute as the sun sank and the big old trees that surrounded the house blocked the solar heat that had been pouring in the windows all afternoon. Thoughtfully, Maggie went to check the radiators, and found them stone cold.

So the war had started, had it?

No doubt, she thought, Karr had planned this little episode. In fact, he might even have turned the boiler off himself, the minute his last cooperative tenants left the house. He hadn't waited long, that was sure, for it would have taken hours for the residual heat in the system to dissipate.

Maggie could imagine him shutting down the boiler and chuckling as he calculated how long it was likely to be before she realized the house was growing colder. Well, if he thought a minor detail like this would make her give in and move, he was going to get a surprise.

It was late April, and not bitterly cold. The walls were thick, and though the temperature in her apartment might be just a bit unpleasant by morning, the worst that could happen was she'd have some unhappy house plants. It would not be dangerous either for her or for Tripp. She'd simply bundle up in a couple of blankets and keep right on working, with hot tea to keep her warm.

Still, since she needed to talk to Chad Buckley anyway...

She caught him just as he was leaving his office, and he listened to her story and clicked his tongue chidingly. "No heat? Now that's downright naughty. You call your landlord right now, and if there's no action overnight, I can file for an injunction in the morning."

"I don't want to call," Maggie objected. "It would only give him satisfaction if I do. He's probably waiting at the office for me to complain."

"Well, you can't expect a judge to take this too seriously if you haven't given proper notification of the problem."

Maggie chewed her lip. "I guess that's so. But with heat or without, I'm not about to leave here."

"As a matter of fact, you shouldn't go to a motel or anything like that," Chad agreed. "If it looks like you've moved out, the whole thing's a moot point."

Karr wasn't in the office. Maggie was almost disappointed in him. She left her name with his answering service and did five minutes' worth of aerobics to get her blood circulating. Then she filled the teakettle and called the pizza delivery service. She'd been craving pizza ever since Karr had caused her to turn the last one into a cinder—what better night to indulge herself with something hot and spicy?

She made her pot of tea, then stripped the down comforter off her bed and dragged it over to the library table. She bunched up a blanket nearby for Tripp, but he seemed taken with the comforter instead. As soon as Maggie settled down at the table again, he crept under the edge of it, propped his chin on her woolly socks and gave a satisfied sigh.

She buried herself in work once more. The main structure of the section was roughed out, but now the really difficult part started. Getting the eight extra pages was a blessing, but even with the additional room, every word was going to have to count. And there was still a pile of manuscripts to read....

Maggie didn't realize how involved she'd gotten till she reached for her cup of tea and found it cold. The pot had lost most of its warmth, as well, and she glanced at the clock above the library table with astonishment, and then a trace of consternation. Her pizza should have come by now, but there had been no buzz from downstairs. She wouldn't put it past Karr to have fiendishly disconnected the doorbells, too—just in case the lack might prove annoying.

Well, she'd just go down and wait. Surely it wouldn't be long now.

Tripp raised his head and growled. Maggie was amused by the way his voice was muffled by the thickness of the comforter, until she heard the indistinct sound that must have caused him to rouse. It sounded like someone was coming slowly up the stairs. But Libby was gone, and the pizza delivery man never came past the main door.

"It's a ghost, no doubt," she mocked. Probably the long-dead original owner of her apartment. He'd waited seventy-odd years to return, and then coincidentally chose the very first night Maggie was alone to start haunting his former home.

Right, she ridiculed herself. And he was a polite ghost, too—for he knocked at the door instead of walking straight on through! She struggled out of the enveloping comforter and fumbled for her wallet.

Tripp escorted her to the door and barked furiously at the sight of Karr with a pizza box balanced on one upraised hand like a waiter's tray.

He made a face at the dog and turned to Maggie. "What's the matter with you? You look like you've seen a... Oh, sorry. I didn't mean to scare you."

"You didn't, particularly. Too bad you didn't think of dragging a few chains along—it would have been much more effective."

He looked interested. "I'll remember that in case I have insomnia and need something to do in the middle of the night."

Maggie said tartly, "I'm glad it takes so little to entertain you."

"Oh, I didn't say haunting was my *favorite* pastime for the wee hours," he began.

"Never mind. May I ask how you happened to end up with my pizza? Isn't your business doing well?" Mock consternation crept into her voice. "Have you had to start moonlighting?"

"As a matter of fact, my business isn't doing quite as well as last week—before I met you. But I haven't taken a second job just yet. I happened to meet the delivery man at the end of the drive, so I offered to save him the trip and bring this up, since I was coming anyway."

"You're so incorrigibly helpful, Karr. You could have just phoned me."

"Oh, no," he said earnestly. "Not when you'd left a special message for me."

"I left my name, that's all."

"That's what I mean. Since you didn't tell the service what it was about, I assumed it must be personal. I wouldn't have bothered you otherwise, you see—I hadn't forgotten my promise to leave you alone till Wednesday. But when you seemed to need me..."

"I need you like a gorilla needs a bodyguard." Maggie took the box out of his hands. "I'll bet you're here because you couldn't stand the suspense. You just had to come out to see the effects of your little experiment."

Karr followed her into the apartment. "What experiment? And what suspense? I decided days ago to expect the worst from you so I'd never have to suffer suspense any more. It saves such a lot of effort, you see."

Maggie was annoyed that he hadn't given himself away. "I mean the little matter of heat," she snapped.

"I was going to ask you about that. Don't you believe in it? It's damned unpleasant in here, and the toupee looks like he has frostbite."

Maggie gritted her teeth. "That's because there is no heat. The boiler seems to have—accidentally, of course—gone on the blink."

Karr looked at her admiringly. "You know, I'll bet when you really get rolling the sarcasm just drips off your tongue. Is that why you called me? I'll be happy to light a fire to keep you warm."

"That wouldn't do much good—the fireplace hasn't worked for years."

The gleam in his eyes was particularly wicked. "Who's talking about fireplaces?"

Maggie choked. If he meant more personal, intimate, *internal* sorts of fires—

The mere implication seemed to warm her blood. She was annoyed to find that she was so suggestible.

"If you'll excuse me a minute," Karr said innocently, "I'll run down and check the boiler out."

Maggie got her breath back, finally. "And correct whatever you did to it?"

He paused at the door, frowning. "What *I* did to it?"

Against her better judgment, Maggie's convictions wavered. Was he really that good an actor? "You didn't?"

"I regret to say the idea of fiddling with the furnace didn't even occur to me. I'll be back in a minute."

Tripp had followed him to the door, and he started barking triumphantly as he realized that he'd finally routed the enemy.

Karr surveyed the dog with distaste. "In the meantime, you might stick the toupee in the oven so he won't chill out completely. About five hundred degrees for half an hour should do it."

"Oh, I'm sure he'll be fine, now that you've got his heart pounding with excitement."

"It was worth a try," Karr muttered.

Maggie put the pizza in the oven instead. This time, remembering what had happened to the last one, she set the timer.

A few minutes later, she was pouring boiling water over a fresh set of tea bags when the radiators began to clatter and bang—a welcome racket that meant steam was once more rising in the pipes.

A couple of minutes later Karr came back. "The pilot light had gone out. I couldn't find any obvious reason for it, but maybe the boiler didn't realize you were still here and decided to take a vacation."

"Or maybe somebody turned it off."

"You've got a nasty cynical twist, haven't you, Rawlings? If I had shut off the pilot light, I'd have made damned sure the gas was off, too."

She blinked. "It wasn't?"

"Nope. That's what took so long—I had to air the basement out before I could relight the boiler, or the whole place could have gone up with a boom."

"Oh," she said, in a very small voice.

The glance he cast at her was casually sympathetic. "Don't panic—it's not likely to happen again. I'll have it checked out tomorrow, but it was probably just a down draft from the wrong direction that blew the flame out. The doors have been open a lot today, I'm sure, with the Montgomerys moving."

That made sense. She'd reasoned herself that the boiler must have quit hours ago. "Thanks," Maggie managed. She felt like a worm for suspecting him. After all, there was no question about her right to stay in the apartment till Wednesday, with all the usual amenities. And he *had* promised to leave her alone till then.

"It's nothing. I certainly wouldn't want the place to blow up with you inside it."

She didn't quite know what to say about that. His voice had a huskier-than-usual edge that actually sounded sincere, and it made her feel just a little shaky inside.

"All the talk of ghosts tonight might give you ideas about spending eternity here," he went on easily, "and then I'd have to deal with you forever."

Maggie glared at him. "You *deserve* to be haunted!"

The oven timer buzzed, and he sniffed appreciatively as Maggie slid the pizza onto the butcher-block counter. "All that food you brought home yesterday," he said, "and you're eating pizza?"

"I didn't feel like cooking." She fought a brief battle with her conscience, and surrendered. He had done her a very good turn tonight—keeping her from being blown up or gassed—and the least she could do was offer to share her pizza. "Would you like some? There's plenty."

Karr hesitated just long enough to make her wonder whether he was suspicious or merely astonished. Then he said, "Sure," and smiled.

It was a slower, warmer and even more heart-rocking smile than Maggie had seen before, and she had to look away in order to fight the sudden all-gone feeling in the pit of her stomach. It wasn't fair, she thought. She didn't even *like* the man....

Don't you? said a little voice at the back of her mind. If she'd met him under other circumstances, and if he wasn't trying to make her leave her home...

But she hadn't, and he was—and that ended the matter, of course. Didn't it?

She put plates and mugs on a tray, and Karr carried the hot pizza pan into the living room. "At least there's the illusion of warmth when one sits in front of a fireplace," he said. "Even an empty one. Are you sure this thing doesn't work?"

"I was told when I moved in that it hadn't been used in twenty years."

"But you didn't try it out for yourself?"

"If you're trying to con me into smoking myself out, it won't work, Karr. You're the one who said there's all kinds of loose brick up there."

"I'd forgotten telling you that. In any case, who wants to carry wood all the way up the stairs? I think my idea for keeping warm was a better one."

His voice was lazy and smooth, lapping over her like warm, soapy water caressing delicate skin. Maggie didn't look at him. She settled down on one of the couches and picked up the teapot. "Personally, I think a gas log would be the best idea of all."

Karr sighed. "Is there really no romance in your soul?"

"No. But there's beer in the refrigerator—you'll have to settle for that."

He laughed. "The tea's fine." He waited till she'd poured, then he picked up the blanket she'd tossed on the floor for Tripp and sat down next to her, tucking the wool throw solicitously around both of them.

Maggie could feel the heat radiating from his body.

She raised an eyebrow at him, and Karr said easily, "Well, since you didn't like my first idea for keeping you warm, this is a compromise. It'll take a while for the boiler to build up enough pressure to push steam all the way up here."

There wasn't any point in protesting, she decided. Whatever she said, he'd have a snappy answer. She'd just make sure he didn't think she was affected in any way. As long as he didn't realize that the warmth of his body seemed to be soaking into her muscles and melting them like jelly over an open flame... Enough, she told herself. She really must keep a little better control of her thoughts.

She tried to sound prim. "It's nice to be warm again."

Karr grinned. "Isn't it, though?" he murmured, and slid an arm around her shoulders.

Maggie leaned forward abruptly and grabbed for the pizza server. She thought Karr smothered a chuckle, but she wasn't certain.

He took the plate she offered almost absentmindedly. "I'm beginning to see why you're a bit choosy about a place to live."

Maggie was astounded. "You are?"

He nodded. "Some of your furniture wouldn't fit just anywhere. How did you get that bed up here, anyway? It's enormous."

Maggie glanced toward the bedroom end of the apartment. It was only dimly lit, and her big canopied bed was little more than a looming shadow. "I haven't any idea," she said. "It was here when I came. The wardrobe and library table and bed belonged to the original owner of this apartment, and they've been sort of passed down from tenant to tenant ever since."

Too late, she wondered if Karr would seize that admission to argue that the pieces didn't really belong to her, and therefore she shouldn't have any trouble finding another place to live, after all.

But he merely asked, "What do you mean, the original owner?"

"Didn't the people you bought the house from tell you anything about its history?"

Karr shrugged. "I didn't ask."

"I guess I'm not surprised." Maggie picked an olive off the top of her pizza and munched it. "The people who built the house lived in it for decades, so their children grew up here. The oldest son never left home—"

"That must have driven his parents nuts." He looked thoughtful. "You know, maybe this place is haunted after all. This tendency of the tenants to drive other people crazy—"

Maggie raised her voice a little and kept talking. "But he wanted his own quarters, so he took over the old attics and servants' quarters and rebuilt them into this." She waved a hand. "From what I hear, he fancied himself a proper gentleman—he was more Edwardian than King Edward himself."

"Eccentric," Karr mused. "That fits the pattern."

Maggie ignored him. "He put in all the walnut paneling, and the bookshelves, and the fireplace. As for the bed, maybe they built it right here. I just wish I could have seen the place with all the original furnishings. I'm sure he had dark green leather armchairs by the fire and sporting prints on the walls and genuine Oriental rugs instead of reproductions." She scuffed one foot on the rug to make her point.

Karr looked around thoughtfully. "The kitchen doesn't seem to fit."

"No, it was done later, when the rest of the house was converted."

"The Edwardian gentleman's desire for independence didn't extend to cooking for himself?"

Maggie laughed. "Apparently not. Too bad—he'd have spared no expense."

"You absolutely love this house, don't you?" It was not really a question. "Tell you what, Maggie, my dear— why don't you buy it from me? It would solve a big problem for both of us."

Especially for him, Maggie thought. He was probably thinking fondly of being rid of a headache named Maggie Rawlings. "Sorry," she said crisply, "but I don't have that sort of cash tucked into a sock under my mattress."

"Now that's a picture worth considering. Is it a black nylon stocking? Or maybe one of those with designs embroidered all the way to the top? Or—"

"I said I *didn't* have— Oh, never mind."

"Well, you think it over. I wouldn't even insist on making a profit."

Maggie studied his face as he reached for another slice of pizza. "If you don't care about a profit, why did you buy it? And if you're not so sure it's a good investment anymore, why on earth would *I* want it? Even if I had the money, I'm not cut out to be a landlord."

"Why rent it? You could have the whole thing to yourself, and nobody could ever bother you again."

"*All* of it? Nobody needs this much space. The original owners probably had ten servants living in to take care of it all."

Karr entered into the game. "And probably two grandmothers, three maiden aunts and a dozen or so permanent houseguests."

Maggie laughed. "Don't forget the eccentric son in the attic!" She reached for the teapot. "I'd better make more tea. This is getting cold."

Before she could rise, Karr caught her hand and drew her against him on the couch. "What is it about this place that's so special to you, Maggie?" he asked.

She'd never heard him sound quite so serious, and the solemn tone of his voice drew the truth from her before she had a chance to wonder if it was wise to tell him. "It's mine," she whispered. "It's the only place I've ever had just for me."

He was silent, and after a moment Maggie grew edgy. Did he think she sounded like a fool?

"I don't know where you grew up, or how," she said quietly, "but I'll bet you had a room of your own, with a door you could close when you wanted to be alone. A place where you could sit and think and dream—"

"And you didn't have that?"

She shook her head. "Not only didn't I have a room, I never had a bed to myself till I was in college. I had to share with one or the other of my stepsisters. We were so poor that sometimes—but you don't want to hear all that.''

He didn't answer.

And I don't want to tell you, Maggie thought. *I don't want to see pity in your eyes, or shock, or distaste.*

"So that's why I like it here," she said, trying to sound cheerful. "It's just right for me."

Karr shook his head. "But then why not jump at the chance to have something of your own—a town house or a condo that nobody could ever force you to leave?"

Maggie gave a cynical laugh, remembering how innocently she had believed in that philosophy once. "As if that could ever be guaranteed! And if the value of the property drops in the meantime... No, thanks, Karr. I decided long ago that I'd be better off paying rent than putting all my eggs in one basket like that." She cleared her throat. "Excuse me. I really want another cup of tea." She pushed the blanket aside and carried the tea tray to the kitchen.

The water was boiling by the time Karr said anything at all, and then he only called, "Are you finished with the pizza?"

Maggie was relieved that he hadn't pursued the subject. "Yes, unless you want the rest."

He didn't answer, just picked up the pan and brought it to the kitchen.

She filled the teapot and turned to set it on the tray. She didn't realize how close Karr was, and she bumped into him, spilling the tea. He caught her by the elbows and steadied her so the hot liquid missed them both.

"Sorry," she said. "I don't usually run over my guests."

He didn't chuckle, and he didn't release her. Slowly his hands tightened on her arms, drawing her closer.

"I don't think—" Maggie began.

His voice was unsteady. "I don't *want* to think." He took the teapot out of her hands and set it down, and put his arms around her.

In the subtle light, his eyes weren't blue any more but almost black. Maggie stared at him, almost hypnotized, until his mouth touched hers with the sudden searing impact of a branding iron. Her eyes fluttered shut then, but it wouldn't have mattered. Her sense of sight and sound almost vanished as she concentrated on the taste and feel of him.

She had never been kissed so thoroughly, so deeply, so completely. Every cell of her body felt the jolt of adrenaline as the power of his touch surged through her, followed by a luxurious lassitude. All she wanted to do was lean against him, to let her body melt into his....

From somewhere deep inside, she managed to dredge up a last fragment of sense. She couldn't push herself away from him—she didn't have enough self-control for that—but she managed to say, against his mouth, "I don't think this is such a wise idea."

His hand slipped to the back of her neck and his long fingers splayed through her hair and pulled her closer yet—too close for another protest even if she'd had the breath or the will to formulate it. He kissed her once more, and then said, with a wry note in his voice, "I know. The last thing we need is more complications. But it sure felt good." He held her a little way from him and looked into her face for a moment that seemed to stretch into forever, and then released her.

Tripp whimpered and pawned at Maggie's ankle, and Karr looked down at him, eyebrows raised. "Now there's a miracle," he said. His voice still didn't sound quite right, Maggie thought. "The toupee didn't bite me. Or was I just so carried away I didn't notice? You're right, Maggie—that was very definitely not a wise idea." He ran a gentle finger along her jaw, from the sensitive spot under her ear to the point of her chin. "Stay warm," he whispered, and was gone.

Maggie sagged against the refrigerator door. Oh, she was warm all right, she thought. It was a wonder she hadn't sizzled into a puddle right there on the kitchen floor.

A cold spring rain fell all day Tuesday. Maggie spent the morning working, and by early afternoon she'd finished one story and blocked out two more. For a change of pace, she decided to dig through the remaining piles of unsolicited manuscripts on the corner of her desk. Only when she slid the first one into the return envelope did she realize she had just one form rejection letter left from the supply she'd brought home from the office.

"An editor without rejection slips is hardly an editor at all," she told Tripp, who had rolled himself up in the kitchen rug. He yawned at her and tucked his chin once more.

She looked out the window at the rain and sighed. If she waited for the rain to stop, the office supply store—the closest source of a photocopy machine—would be closed. A little dampness wouldn't do her any harm, she supposed, and the fresh air and the walk down the lane would do her good.

Today she'd have almost welcomed the sight of a black Mercedes coming up the drive, but it didn't appear, and Maggie was well dampened by the time she climbed on the bus. It was raining even harder when she got off, and the bottom six inches of her jeans were wet before she reached the office supply store.

Never had she missed her car so much. Life would be so much easier if she didn't have to depend on public transportation.

She was still at the copy machine, waiting for it to churn out fifty copies of her letter, when Karr came in, shaking a few drops of water from his raincoat.

"I thought I saw you splashing across the street," he said.

Maggie supposed it was inevitable that she'd run into him on this expedition. It was just regrettable he'd showed up too late to keep her from a good soaking. But since she'd been half-expecting him to turn up all along, she told herself there was really no reason for the warm, unsettled feeling in the pit of her stomach. It had only been a kiss, after all....

And donkeys fly, too, a little voice in the back of her brain murmured.

Her gaze seemed magnetically attracted to Karr's mouth, and the unsteadiness inside her grew as she recalled the way he had kissed her last night.

That was probably why he'd done it, she thought—in order to knock her judgment all awry. If she was wise, she wouldn't let him guess he'd succeeded.

"I see your radar's still in working order," she murmured. The copy machine whirred and stopped, and she gathered her copies.

"Oh, yes. That's never been in doubt." His voice was low and intimate. "You're not having any trouble staying warm, I trust?"

Maggie was startled for a second, until she realized he was referring to the boiler. He certainly couldn't know that she felt as if she was going to burst into flame at any moment. "No trouble at all." It took effort to sound calm. "Though as long as we're talking about the house, the water pressure still isn't anything to brag about."

"Sorry," he said. He didn't sound it. "I can't possibly do anything about that today. And since tomorrow's Wednesday, and you'll be moving, it's hardly worth bothering."

She stepped up to the register and waited for the cashier to add up her purchases. "You'll have to fix the water sometime," she chided, "if you're ever going to rent those apartments again. Why not take care of the problem right now?"

"Who says I'm going to rent them?" He sounded honestly curious.

Maggie was too stunned to answer. The cashier had to remind her to take her change. She dropped it heedlessly in the pocket of her trenchcoat. "Aren't you?" she asked.

Karr took her arm and guided her easily toward the door. They were outside, under the minimal protection of the awning, before he said, "If I was, Maggie, why would I have gone to so much trouble and expense to get everyone to move out?" His tone was almost gentle, as if he was explaining the obvious to a child. There was none of the banter she'd grown so used to hearing from him, and that scared her.

"Because the current crop of tenants are hardly the kind you'll be looking for after you renovate the place," she said. "None of us are exactly in the market for upscale housing, after all, and if you only have half as many apartments to rent after the renovation's done—"

It was a case of diminishing returns, she reflected. Why hadn't that occurred to her before? To create the luxurious apartments that would command luxurious rents called for a very expensive renovation. But with fewer tenants to pay the costs, it would be difficult for Karr to recoup the kind of investment that Eagle's Landing needed. It could only pay for itself if he ended up with thirty or forty apartments instead of half a dozen, and the house, huge as it was, didn't have space enough for that.

But there could be more, she realized. How could she have forgotten that Eagle's Landing wasn't just a building, but a strip of land that would be the perfect setting for another of his long rows of town houses? If he tore out the trees, filled the lake, paved the ground, there'd be room for a hundred town houses—or perhaps fifty larger, more elaborate, more expensive ones. No wonder Karr had said something to Dan Montgomery about the demand for upscale housing.

Maggie's voice was practically a shriek. "You're going to tear it down and build more of those awful little boxes?"

Karr put his hands in the pockets of his trench coat. "I didn't say I was going to do anything of the sort," he pointed out.

"You're always very careful not to say anything at all! I suppose next you'll expect me to believe you're going to remodel it and move in yourself!"

The suggestion seemed to strike his fancy. "Now that's something to consider."

Maggie was disgusted. "Oh, come on, Karr. The idea of you rattling around in that enormous house playing lord of the manor is utterly ridiculous, and you know it."

"But you're the one who brought it up," he protested. "Where do you live now?"

"In one of the town houses. And as a matter of fact I like it just fine there. Which reminds me, we closed deals on three condos and two more town houses over the weekend, so—"

"I'm not worried."

His eyes began to sparkle. "Oh, neither am I, any more. But perhaps I should warn you, darling—at the rate they're going, if you wait much longer your only option will be to move in with me."

CHAPTER FIVE

KARR offered her a ride, but Maggie—still in shock at the idea that Eagle's Landing would soon be nothing more than a heap of broken brick and slate—didn't think she could rely on willpower to keep her silence on the subject. And she knew better than to tear into him before she'd had a chance to think. Karr had had time to consider every angle, and he would have no trouble countering any argument she might make. No, it would be far better to consider her options and sort out a plan of attack before she acted.

That she *would* do something about the problem wasn't in question. Suddenly the whole affair had become more than a matter of her own inconvenience, and she couldn't square it with her conscience to simply stand by. Eagle's Landing might have a worn-out roof, falling chimneys, an unreliable boiler and peeling paint, but that didn't mean it deserved to be crumbled into dust and replaced with a row of town houses.

The thought of town houses reminded her of Libby, who'd probably be every bit as upset as Maggie was over this. Perhaps she'd have some ideas.

Maggie stopped at the florist shop on the corner and walked up to Karr's town house development.

She couldn't remember if Libby had ever mentioned her new house having a number, and the long row of almost-identical front doors was a daunting sight. There was a mailbox beside every door—but was she really going to have to climb the three steps to each infinitesimal front porch and read the label on every box till she found the Montgomerys? And what if Libby and Dan hadn't yet gotten around to putting their name on the mailbox?

The rain was growing heavier, which made it harder to see. Maggie tucked her cellophane-wrapped sheaf of flowers under the edge of her raincoat and started trudging down the row of houses. First she passed a garage, set back from the street at the end of a drive, then the impersonal front of a house—with a teal green front door and "Adams" on the mailbox—then another garage, and another house...

Near the third front door was a small but highly visible sign marking it as the sales office, and Maggie hesitated only a second before she went in. On her own, she'd be all night finding Libby. She needed all the help she could get.

A well-dressed brunette looked up from a desk just inside the front door with a friendly smile. "May I help you?"

"I'm looking for a resident—"

Karr came down the stairs, wearing his raincoat. "Well, hello, Maggie. Did you turn down a ride because you didn't want to tell me you were coming here? Can I show you around, or would you rather look on your own?"

I should have known he'd be back in the office by now, Maggie thought. If that wasn't just her luck! "Oh, I'm only interested in one model—the Wakefield, I think it is." Wasn't that the one he'd said was sold out?

Karr didn't miss a beat. "We'll be building more of those soon."

At Eagle's Landing, of course. Maggie had to bite her tongue to keep from snapping at him.

"And I'll happily put your name on the waiting list. But if you need alternative housing in the meantime, the offer I made is still open." His voice was almost a caress.

The receptionist turned to Karr with a puzzled look, obviously wondering what he was up to, and Maggie felt warm color washing over her face. What was the matter with her, she wondered irritably. The first time he'd made the idiotic suggestion that she move in with him, she'd ignored it—but of course, that hadn't been in front of his employees.

His gaze rested speculatively on her face. "Well, well," he said gently. "I had no idea you could turn such an interesting color. It's very attractive."

Maggie was furious with herself. She'd long ago learned not to react to suggestive comments, public or private—but what was there about Karr Elliot that seemed to knock out all her defenses?

"As a matter of fact, I don't need anything but directions," she said coolly. "I'm bringing a house-warming gift to my friend Libby, but if I have to wander around among all these identical *units* till I find the right one, the flowers will be dead."

"I'll walk you over," Karr said. He handed the receptionist a folder.

"Directions are too hard to follow, then?" Maggie asked politely as he held the door for her.

Karr's eyebrows rose a fraction. "Good try, but you're not going to maneuver me into admitting anything of the sort."

"Oh—that's a relief. I thought perhaps you had to have a crew come in every morning to gather up people who've been lost all night and were still trying to find their way home."

Karr paused on the tiny porch to raise an umbrella, and held it over her head. "Not at all. I happen to be going home, and my town house is in the same direction as Libby's. But even if it wasn't, I'd leap at the chance to spend a few minutes walking in the rain with you."

"Right," Maggie muttered, and Karr smiled.

Halfway down the long row of town houses, he pointed to an apricot-colored door and swept her a dramatic bow. "If you'd like to stop by for a cappuccino when you're finished, I'm in number thirty. In fact, I owe you a meal—"

"I'll keep it in mind. But don't wait up for me."

"It would be a pleasure," he murmured, and watched from the sidewalk till she was safely on the tiny porch.

There was already a heart-shaped wreath on Libby's door, a delicate thing woven of wheat and silk flowers. And the name was lettered proudly on the mailbox, too.

Libby answered the bell and whooped with delight. "Maggie, I'm so glad to see you! Come in, I want you to see what we've already done." Her hair was wrapped in a scarf, and there was a smudge of what looked like newspaper ink on her nose. Maggie thought she had never looked happier.

Maggie followed her across the foyer. The tiny space was dim and a little gloomy today, especially in the upper corners of the staircase, but she could imagine it with sunshine streaming in the glass panels beside the door.

The living room was larger than she'd expected. Beyond it was the dining alcove. Boxes were scattered over the floor in both areas, half-unpacked, but there were already pictures on the walls and throw pillows on the couch. It looked as if the Montgomerys were wasting no time in settling in.

Libby pushed several boxes aside so they could walk through. "I was just going to take a coffee break," she said. "And you look as if you could use one, too—you're soaked through. What brings you out on such a rotten day?"

"Errands," Maggie said. "Besides, I missed you." She handed over the flowers. "This isn't your real house-warming gift, of course. I'm waiting till you get settled and find out what you need—but it looks as if you're doing very well.''

Libby turned the coffeepot on and put the flowers in water. ''I suppose you mean it's something of a miracle that I can already find a vase, but I've simply got to get it all done before I start work next week. Now, really—what brings you out on a day like this, Maggie?'' She set two mugs of coffee on the kitchen table and pulled out a chair.

''Well, it started out to be errands,'' Maggie admitted. ''Then I found out Karr's going to tear down Eagle's Landing and build town houses or condos or something there instead.''

Libby's eyebrows went up. ''Really?''

''Isn't that perfectly revolting?'' Maggie paced the width of the kitchen. ''How many housing developments does Eagleton need, anyway?''

''I suppose it makes sense. When the new high-speed commuter line's built next year, it'll be easier to get back and forth to the city, so we'll get another surge of people moving this direction with money to spend on housing.''

''I hadn't even thought of that,'' Maggie admitted. ''They've been promising that line so long I'd stopped counting on it ever being built. But even with better train service, it will still be a pain to get downtown from here.''

''You do it regularly.''

''But I can choose when I travel, and I don't have to go every day,'' Maggie pointed out. ''That's a lot different from riding a train every rush hour.''

''I know. Commuting isn't my favorite activity, either, but there are plenty of people who would do it—especially if they could live in a nice community, in a new town house.''

''That doesn't mean they have to be built at Eagle's Landing.''

Libby shrugged. "Why not? As a house, it's a white elephant, but it's only a mile outside town, and there must be several acres of land."

"You sound as if you approve!"

Libby reached for the coffeepot and topped off their mugs. "There are certain realities in the world, Maggie, and one of them is that Eagle's Landing is never going to be the way we used to know it."

"That doesn't mean it should be destroyed. As long as I thought Karr was just going to remodel, that was one thing. But tearing it down is just too much. There have to be laws about things like this." Maggie toyed with her mug, frowning. "I know—there are preservation people who can stop him. We did an article last year about a national group that steps in and prevents wanton destruction of landmarks."

Libby looked doubtful. "Maybe—if you can convince them it's a landmark. But it's a little late for that, don't you think?"

"Well, since I can't turn the clock back and start last week, now is the only time I've got." She checked her watch. "I can call this afternoon and get things started."

"There are battles you can't win, Maggie, and old buildings that aren't worth saving."

"Eagle's Landing isn't one of them," Maggie said stubbornly. "And I'm not going to stand by and see it destroyed in order to build more of *these*." She caught herself and bit her lip. "I'm sorry. I'm not insulting your new house, honestly. Will you show me around?"

"Of course." Libby set her mug down and led the way. "It's going to take time to get everything just the way I want it. I don't know what to do about curtains and wallpaper. And the odd space in the foyer needs a table, but where am I going to find one that'll fit?"

Maggie had to admit to some surprise at the sense of privacy and quiet. The arrangement of the houses with garages between not only made it seem as if each house stood alone. It also allowed the upper floor to have windows on all sides, unlike most town house developments, so the bedrooms were light and airy. The bathroom was nice, as well, big and well-designed. In fact, she'd have called the whole house attractive, except that would be a compliment to Karr, and she was darned if she'd go quite that far.

And everything seemed reasonably well-built, too. The trim was nicely finished, the floors were level, nothing creaked.

Of course, it was easy to make things look good when they were brand-new, she reflected. The condo she'd fallen in love with three years ago had been almost as appealing, even in its half-finished state....

It would be interesting, she thought, to see how these houses stood up to the test of time. She'd bet in twenty years they'd be sagging and twisting, while Eagle's Landing would still be standing straight and every bit as solid as it was today....

But it wouldn't, of course. It wouldn't be standing at all, unless Maggie could stop the destruction.

"It's very nice, Libby," she said when the tour was over. "I mean it. And when you've had a chance to decorate, it'll be lovely."

"It won't be too long till it's finished, I hope. Dan and I've agreed that my paycheck will go directly toward the house for a while."

"I'd forgotten—you said when I first came that you're starting to work, but I was so preoccupied I didn't even ask about it. Where will you be working? What are you going to do?"

Libby looked at her feet as if she regretted bringing up the subject. "At Elliot Development," she said finally.

Her voice was so soft that Maggie had to strain to hear, but the impact of her words was like a blow in the stomach. "You're joking. Libby, you can't be planning to work for Elliot the Great!"

Libby's head came up. "I start just as soon as possible," she said firmly. "And as soon as I've had some training, I'll probably be selling those town houses, or condos, or whatever he's planning to build out at Eagle's Landing."

Maggie was still in shock by the time she got home.

Talk about your basic bad decision, she told herself derisively. She'd told Libby every thought in her head—and Libby would no doubt turn straight around and tell Karr.

Not that she blamed Libby for thinking it was her duty as Karr's employee to inform him of the threat. If Maggie had been in her friend's shoes, she might have done the same thing. But it certainly made matters more difficult. By the time the preservation people could get started, Karr would be three steps ahead of them.

Still, she had to try, so she dug through her old files till she found the phone number of the preservation society. When she asked for the person she'd interviewed for the magazine, she almost held her breath—the story had run almost two years ago, and the woman she'd talked to might not be with the organization any more.

But the young man who answered the phone was cheerful. "Oh, yes, she still works here. But she's in Virginia just now, picketing a developer. I'm her assistant. Can I help you?"

Maggie was doubtful. He sounded very young, and when she told him her story, he was clearly unenthusiastic. "I don't know, Miss Rawlings. If the architect's unknown and the original owners weren't noteworthy or infamous..."

"It's a great house."

He sighed and suddenly sounded much older. "They all are, aren't they? The problem is, we're spread so thin right now that we may not even have the resources to look into it. But hey, give me the details, and I'll tell my boss about it when she gets back."

It was better than nothing, Maggie supposed. "When will that be?"

"Well, they're only getting started, so I'd guess three weeks or so."

Maggie wailed, "But that will be too late! Isn't there something that can be done in the meantime?"

"Oh, there are a bunch of things you can do on the local level. I'll send you our handbook on how to get started. In the meantime, is there a local preservation group? Or a historical society or something?"

"Not that I've ever heard of."

"Well, then, the first step is to organize one. Or you can call a public meeting and start getting the neighborhood informed and aroused—that works sometimes."

But there isn't really a neighborhood, Maggie thought. Eagle's Landing was so secluded that the tenants themselves had been the only neighbors. And it wouldn't be easy to rouse support for her cause, either. If Libby's reaction was any indication, a good many of the people of Eagleton would feel that trading one deteriorating old house for an entire new development wasn't a bad bargain.

"Get the mayor on your side," the young man recommended. "And as a last-ditch stand, if you can get onto the property, you can stage some sort of takeover or sit-in."

"That's sort of what I'm doing right now," Maggie said. She put down the phone with a feeling of doom. Doing research, writing reports, organizing groups, conducting long talks with city officials—none of that was going to fit into her calendar, not if she had to juggle it along with her regular work. If only the special edition hadn't come along just now...

Which of course was nonsense. She'd planned for that project for a year, looked forward to it, dreamed of it. And she'd be enjoying every minute of the work on it, too, if it wasn't for Karr.

"Damn Karr Elliot," she muttered, and reached for her notebook calendar. She could at least try to get the ball rolling. She'd search through her list of contacts to see if she knew anybody who might have connections at Eagleton's city hall, and perhaps they'd take over....

The notebook had been lying atop her answering machine, hiding the blinking red light. What now, she thought with foreboding. Karr, reminding her that she now had just twenty-four hours left of her thirty days?

Probably not, she thought. He'd be far more subtle than that—he'd be more likely to send the message with a bunch of balloons, or as a singing telegram....

She flicked the switch, and the sultry voice of her editorial assistant filled the room. "Hi, it's Carol. I hope you haven't decided to take your work and go to Acapulco for the week, because Brian's called a progress meeting for the special edition tomorrow morning at ten. That's Wednesday, in case you're really out of touch. Oh, and it's your turn to bring the bagels. Want me to take care of it?"

Maggie groaned. "Why does he think I work at home?" she asked Tripp, who was waiting by the door, obviously hoping for a walk. "It's to avoid all the blasted time-wasting meetings!"

A progress meeting, however, meant that she'd better be able to show significant progress. If she settled down right now, she could have another story finished by dinnertime.

So much for Eagle's Landing, she decided reluctantly. It would have to wait till tomorrow.

It was warm enough on Wednesday morning to put her wools away and dress in a spring suit instead. After a couple of days in jeans and sweaters, the sensual blend of linen and silk felt good against Maggie's skin. And after months of wearing wintry colors, the icy pastel green was a boost to her spirits, as well.

She was in the grassy area near the house, trying to convince Tripp to give up the idea of chasing a particularly tempting squirrel, when the black Mercedes came up the drive.

Karr got out and crossed the grass toward her. Tripp froze in his tracks and started to growl. Maggie scolded him, and he settled at her feet, still growling deep in his throat.

"I see the alarm system is back in order," Karr said. "It must have been the cold that slowed him down the other night."

Maggie had no trouble remembering which night he meant—when he had kissed her and Tripp hadn't jumped to the defense. She shrugged. "Everybody has an off day now and then."

Karr's gaze swept over her, appraising the pastel suit, seeming to linger at her hemline.

The skirt was inches shorter than anything she'd worn through the winter. Trust Karr to notice that first, Maggie thought.

"This certainly isn't one of your off days. You're going to work, I see."

"I work every day," Maggie corrected. "But I'm headed for the office today, if that's what you mean."

"You didn't stop for that cappuccino yesterday."

"I told you not to count on me."

He was watching her closely, as if he intended to sculpt her face. "You can't avoid this forever, Maggie. Today's the deadline."

She looked at the house. From this angle, the heavy brick walls seemed to soar to the sky, so solid and massive that it seemed impossible they could ever be destroyed. "Why are you tearing it down, Karr? There are so many wonderful things about this house—"

He sighed. "It's a business decision. Can't you get that through your head?"

"Destroying it would be a sin!"

He said, suspiciously, "*Would be*? What are you plotting now, Maggie?"

She tossed her hair and started for the door, tugging at Tripp's leash. "To steal a line from you, Mr. Elliot—maybe when it's all over I'll take you out for coffee someday and tell you about it. I have to go or I'll miss my train."

"I'll take you to the station."

"I'm not sure I want you to," she said honestly.

"Why? Are you afraid you might hear something that hurts?"

She put her chin up. "If that's a challenge, I accept it." She took Tripp upstairs, gave him a last petting and a rawhide chew to keep him company and picked up her briefcase.

Karr was waiting beside the Mercedes, the passenger door already open. "In your opinion," he asked as she got in, "exactly which wonderful things about Eagle's Landing will I be condemned to eternal damnation for destroying?" He closed the door and walked around to slide under the wheel.

Maggie watched him warily. Just what was he up to now? He'd sounded almost casual, and yet there had to be an angle. "All of it," she said finally.

"Come on, Maggie. Broken slate, rotting overhangs and all?"

"Those things can be fixed."

"Not easily. And that's not what I asked, anyway. If you're talking about doors and mantels and leaded-glass windows—"

"Of course I am."

"Then let me assure you those things will be saved. I've already made arrangements with a salvage company—"

"That's not good enough, Karr."

He didn't pause. "And, if we have time, we'll save them."

"What do you mean, if you have time? Is this just another argument to get me to move out?"

"I don't *need* another argument. The one I already have is perfectly good. I don't know what you've got up your sleeve, but let me warn you. Leave me alone, and all the really valuable things in this house will be saved."

"Is that supposed to be some kind of consolation prize?" Maggie's voice was bitter. "I don't see that you're making a big concession, anyway—there's a good market for that sort of stuff, and nobody's ever said you didn't have an eye for a profitable deal."

Karr ignored her protest. "But at the first hint of trouble, I'll bring in a wrecking ball and turn the whole house into rubble—and all those wonderful treasures you're so concerned about will be at the bottom of the heap."

Maggie gasped. She felt as if her breath had stuck in her chest.

The Mercedes had pulled up at the train station before she'd regained her voice. She stared straight ahead and said tightly, "You can't knock it down with me inside it."

Karr leaned across her to open the door, then took her chin in the palm of his hand and turned her face to his. His voice was low and husky, but there wasn't a hint of hesitation. "Don't tempt me, Maggie, my dear."

Maggie sat well back in her chair as the editor described the results of a stepped-up sales campaign. She was only half-listening, for it wasn't really her concern whose ads filled the pages, as long as those ads paid the costs of the editorial section.

She was thinking about Karr and the way he'd issued that final threat. If he'd shouted, or gotten red in the face, or sworn at her, she wouldn't have been nearly so disturbed. But instead he'd almost *whispered*, and Maggie didn't know what to think. The only thing she was certain of was that it was even more important that she stay exactly where she was....

She was so absorbed in her own worries that she took a moment even to react to the editor's bombshell.

"I'm sorry to do this to you all," Brian said, "but all the deadlines for the issue have been moved up a week."

Maggie's pencil slid out of her hand. "Brian, that's impossible!"

"Difficult, maybe, but it can't be impossible, because we're going to do it. And before you tell me how unreasonable it is, Rawlings, let me explain the facts of life. You wanted an additional eight pages for editorial content, and you got it. But that pushes the printers to their limit, and they want an extra week or they won't guarantee we'll hit the newsstands on time. If you'd rather have the time and not the space—"

Maggie bit her tongue for an instant. "Forget I said anything, Brian."

"Good. The deadline is now three weeks from to-morrow. Anybody with problems in meeting that, see me after the meeting. I think that's all for this morning. We'll have another progress meeting next Wednesday."

Maggie was the last one out of the room, and she almost bumped into Chad Buckley near Carol's desk. She pulled up short and said eagerly, "Have you found anything out?"

"About your lease? I'm working on it. How's the heat? Since I didn't hear from you—"

"I'm sorry, I should have called you. Elliot the Great turned it on. But it's even more important now that I stay there. How long will it take to evict me, once he starts proceedings?"

Carol sat up straight. "Elliot the Great being the landlord? This sounds interesting, Maggie. Do tell—what have you been doing to get evicted? Loud parties? Loads of men? And most important, if that's what's been going on, why haven't I been invited?"

"It's nothing that interesting," Maggie said crisply.

Chad shrugged. "I can hold it up for weeks, certainly. Months, perhaps. I'll start to work on it."

"If I can just get through this special issue, then I'll have time to fight the real battle. How much do you know about historic preservation?"

"Saving old buildings from the wreckers? I've always been on the other side of that argument, I'm afraid." He smiled a little. "Maybe we should go someplace historic for the weekend, so we could do some research on the question."

"Can't. My attorney told me not to leave home."

Chad shook his head. "Caught in my own advice." He turned as the editor called his name. "See you later, Margaret."

"If you want my opinion, Maggie," Carol said, "free legal advice is worth exactly what you pay for it."

"Except Chad's isn't exactly free," Maggie agreed. She reached for a bagel from the box on Carol's desk. "Thanks for taking care of the snacks. I owe you."

"You certainly do—I'm holding out for that recommendation you promised. Tell me more about your landlord."

"There aren't any fascinating details, I'm afraid. Listen, if Chad comes back before I get away from here, hit the intercom button and I'll slide under my desk— so you can honestly tell him you haven't seen me anywhere."

Chad didn't disturb her, but there were a million other details awaiting Maggie's attention, and it was midafternoon before she could once more pack up her briefcase and take the train to Eagleton.

Even then, she had trouble settling down to work. The rhythmic clacking of wheels against rails seemed to mimic the questions that were going around and around in her mind. What was she to do about Eagle's Landing? Somewhere, there had to be an answer, if she could just find the right person, ask the right question, press the right button.

But that would take time, and how was she to find the necessary hours? The special issue had to come first, especially with the new and more stringent deadline. She wouldn't dare take chances with her job, even if this hadn't been a project close to her heart.

It didn't appear that Chad was going to be much help, either. The only thing of real value he'd had to offer so far was to tell her not to leave the premises.

It was not a good day to be away from home, she realized. When she got to Eagle's Landing, she might find all her possessions neatly stacked in the driveway.

No, Karr had said he'd give her till dark on Wednesday, and she didn't think he'd go back on his offer. But as for what might happen *after* dark ... that was anyone's guess.

The house was quiet. There was not so much as a workman's van around, and certainly no black Mercedes.

Upstairs, Tripp greeted her with frantic yelps. The poor baby must have felt abandoned, Maggie realized. She hadn't realized it, but with no Libby to come and play and take him out for walks, without even the companionable noises from the other apartments that must have assured him throughout every day that he wasn't alone in the world—no wonder he was distraught. It had been cruel not to anticipate how lonely he'd be.

She petted him for a long time, murmuring apologies and reassurances, till he stopped quivering, and then took him out for a walk in the grounds.

It was almost dark by then, and the moon was rising. Maggie found herself thinking that Eagle's Landing would make a perfect haunted house—it wouldn't be hard at all to make the looming facade look threatening, or to create ghostly shadows behind the blank glass of the windows. Only the top floor was an island of sanity, where cheerful yellow light glowed invitingly.

With the downstairs apartments empty except for a few tools, the workmen hadn't bothered to close and lock the doors. Maggie walked through the main floor rooms with Tripp padding at her heels. Moonlight was an inadequate guide—details vanished, while major architectural elements were magnified by the stark lighting—but she could see well enough to make her way around the once-majestic rooms.

Her footsteps echoed on the parquet floor of the entrance hall. Tripp whined once, and the sound seemed to bounce off every wall in the entire house, magnifying till it seemed like the rusty groan of the ghost who could so believably be a part of Eagle's Landing.

Though Maggie had lived by herself for three years, she couldn't recall ever being so totally alone. There was always someone nearby—a neighbor down the hall, a stranger on the street, a co-worker in the office. That was close enough. She was never ill at ease with her own company, and silence was one of her favorite sounds.

But this was different. For the first time in her life, the sense of loneliness overpowered her. It wasn't that she was afraid, for she was used to being on her own. But she knew exactly how Tripp must have felt today, closed up in a silent house, as solitary as if there was no other living being within reach.

And she was just as alone in her effort to save Eagle's Landing. No doubt there were people who would agree with her that the house should not be destroyed—but finding those people, rousing them and inspiring them to action would be up to Maggie. It all came back to her, for no one else seemed to be getting excited about Karr's plans—and by now half of Eagleton must have an inkling of what he was going to do.

Maybe Libby was right, and there were some buildings that couldn't be saved, some battles that couldn't be won. Eagle's Landing was too big for a single family, too small to be efficient as apartments. Perhaps it was simply unsuited to modern use. Perhaps Maggie was wasting her energy in trying—energy she didn't have to spare.

And if she tried and failed—if Karr got a hint of what she was doing—then it would all be lost, and nothing of Eagle's Landing would survive to be used again.

Maggie stood in the old kitchen for a while, watching the angle of the moonlight move slowly across the checkerboard tile floor.

"I'm sorry," she whispered.

In the answering silence was a warmth, as if the house had said, *I understand.*

Then Maggie climbed the stairs, looked up Elliot Development once more in the telephone book and dialed the number.

LIONHEARTED

In the answering silence was everything in it the noise and road. A hideous road.

Then Maggie clicked the return button and Elliot
The colormen mornamon it the telephone book and chance the printed.

CHAPTER SIX

THE office was closed, so Maggie left a message with the answering service operator, who said she'd do her best to get a message to Mr. Elliot and added doubtfully that it might be morning before he called in.

"He's on a heavy date, no doubt," Maggie told Tripp as she put a salmon steak under the broiler.

While it cooked, she phoned Libby to tell her she'd decided not to pursue the historic preservation route after all, and they were still talking when a beep on the line told her she had another call waiting.

She told Libby goodbye and glanced at the clock. It had been only a matter of minutes—her salmon still wasn't done. "Perhaps I was a little unjust about Mr. Elliot's plans for the evening," she murmured as she clicked the button to take her second call.

Tripp snorted, and Maggie laughed.

"You sound as if you're having a good time," Karr said. "Are you in interesting company?"

Maggie reached down to pat the dog. "Of course. And you?"

"Now I am," he murmured. There was something different tonight about the husky edge Maggie had grown used to in his voice. It was every bit as sexy, and it could still send a little thrill up her spine, but...

"Maggie?" he said. "The answering service said you wanted me."

She realized what the change was. She was hearing the slight reverberation of a cellular phone. She wasted just an instant wondering where he was. "Yes, I did. I half-expected you'd be here waiting for me when I got home tonight.''

"I considered it." He sounded lazy, as if he was stretched out on a lounge chair on a warm beach with his eyes closed and a cold drink in his hand. "But I decided I'd said everything there was to say, so I made other plans for my evening."

In the background, Maggie could hear the soft murmur of a feminine voice. Maybe she hadn't been so far wrong after all—she suspected Karr was quite capable of flirting on the phone with one woman while in the company of another. "Well, I'm sorry to upset your date."

"You'd better be. There's a steak coming off the grill in about two minutes, and I'm not letting it get cold. What's up?"

"I wanted to talk to you about my plans."

"Why right now? This morning you weren't too eager to chat."

"I've had all day to think about things. And I have a proposal for you."

Karr's voice warmed. "But this is so sudden, darling. Are you sure we know each other well enough? Oh, you don't mean that sort of proposal. Okay, shoot."

"There's no reason we can't make a deal. I don't have time right now to move, so—"

"I seem to recall you've said that before. Is there any particular reason I should listen more closely now?"

"I told you about the special project I'm working on. It just got more critical—"

"That is hardly *my* problem."

"Listen, Karr, I'm only giving you an explanation because you asked for one. The fact is, there's still the little matter of the thirty days' notice that I didn't get. My attorney says I've got an excellent case." Her conscience tingled a little at the exaggeration, but she ignored it.

"So either we agree on some terms that let me stay here till I've finished that project, or I will fight eviction. But either way, I'm not moving out till my work's done."

"Perhaps it's escaped your notice, but I don't have to negotiate with you, Maggie."

"But if you're smart, you will. You see, if we have an agreement, I can relax and concentrate on work, and I'll be done in no more than three weeks."

"And what am I supposed to be doing for all that time?"

"Don't tell me there isn't plenty of work to be done around here before you can start building."

"Right—and that includes taking the roof down over your lovely head."

"It's only three weeks, Karr. I'm sure you can rearrange the schedule."

"I'm glad you know so much about my business. So far, I don't see that I'm getting anything out of this little deal of yours."

"Of course you are. You're getting my cooperation."

"Maggie, you don't have a clue what the word means!"

"I promise that the moment my work is done, I'll move—quietly, with no hassle. And since I don't particularly like your town houses or condos or apartments anyway, I'll find somewhere else to live, and you won't even have to put up with me for the rest of my lease, much less afterward." There was a long moment of silence. Maggie's palms were damp. She rubbed them down the legs of her jeans. "Karr? Aren't you going to say anything?"

"I can't. I'm speechless with heartbreak that you didn't like Libby's town house."

"Don't change the subject."

"What do you mean? *I'm* not changing the subject!" He sounded indignant. "You're the one who brought up town houses."

"And you know perfectly well that's not really what I'm talking about. If you don't agree to let me stay, I'll fight. My attorney's already doing the paperwork." Karr didn't know there was no flexibility in the deadline for the special issue, she reasoned, and added, "I must warn you, though. If I have to take time out for strategy sessions and court appearances, my work could drag out for—oh, six to eight weeks instead of only three."

"Or, if I'm particularly annoying, even longer?"

"I made no such threat," Maggie pointed out. "But I'd say that's entirely up to you. What about it? Is it a deal?"

"Let's start once more from the beginning, Margaret. I don't have to negotiate with you."

"Don't you have any sense of fair play? All I'm asking is essentially what you gave every other resident of Eagle's Landing—"

"Oh, no. You've already had—"

"They got a full month's notice. I got less than a week. All I want is the rest of my time, and I'm going to get it one way or the other, Karr."

He sighed. "Look, Maggie, I'll talk to you in the morning."

"Good. I'm very glad you're sensible enough to take some time to think it over."

A hint of laughter crept into his voice. "Oh, I didn't say I was going to think it over. But my steak's done now, and I did warn you that I'm not going to let it get cold. Talk to you tomorrow, sweetheart."

The telephone clicked in her ear.

Well, Maggie thought, she'd done everything she could to be reasonable. It was up to Karr, now, to decide which way they would play out the game.

* * *

The lovely warmth of the day had continued into the evening, so Maggie had opened the windows beside her bed to let in the soft spring air. The fresh breeze flowing over her all night seemed to have washed away all her cares. She was just rousing from a last and most pleasant dream when a roar like a hundred race car engines ripped through the apartment.

She sat up straight, too nearly asleep to know whether she was hearing a dental drill, a fire alarm, a tornado siren ... But as soon as consciousness returned, she recognized the sound. It was a chain saw, and it was up close and personal.

She leaped out of bed, shrieking as her bare feet hit the cold wood floor. Snug in her warm bed, she hadn't realized that overnight the temperature had dropped, and she could almost feel her veins constricting as cold air washed over her. Her white satin nightshirt was no protection at all.

But she didn't close the windows. Instead, she leaned out to see what was going on. She found herself almost face to face with a workman. He was standing in the bucket of a lift truck, half-hidden by the leaves of the huge old oak tree, his chain saw idling. His eyes widened a little when he saw her, but he said, "Good morning, ma'am," and touched two fingers politely to the brim of his hard hat. He raised the saw, and the pitch of the chain saw deepened as it bit into the big branch closest to the house, the one that rubbed against the brick and soothed her to sleep sometimes.

Tree trimming, Maggie thought groggily. She wouldn't have expected that pruning the oak trees would be at the top of Karr's list of things that needed doing around Eagle's Landing. Why would he care about a branch bumping into a wall that he intended to tear down anyway?

Then logic dawned, and she shook her head in disgust as she remembered how carefully he'd studied her apartment the night she'd shared her pizza. He knew perfectly well that branch was right outside her bedroom window, and he'd no doubt considered the effect the noise of a chain saw would have on his one unwelcome tenant at seven in the morning.

So much for her offer of a compromise. It was obvious Karr had made his decision, and it was going to be war.

Maggie decided she wasn't going to give him the satisfaction of making a fuss. It wouldn't take long to trim the offending branch, and as soon as the chain saw stopped and she could hear herself think again, she'd call Chad and tell him to spare no effort in pursuing her case.

She stretched, yawned and reached for the window to close it, only to see the workman standing still and staring at her, his eyes about to pop.

Maggie grabbed for the hemline of her white satin nightshirt. She'd forgotten that when she raised her arms the outfit was barely decent. Of course, on the top floor she didn't have a lot of trouble with window peekers.

"Be careful not to saw off your arm," she advised, and slammed the window, drawing the blinds tight.

The chain saw revved once more. Maggie pulled on a pair of jeans and a turtleneck sweater and retreated to the kitchen to make a pot of coffee. A little caffeine would make it much easier to endure the morning.

Tripp scrambled out of his bed in the corner of the kitchen and went to the door, whining to go out.

Maggie regarded him with just a touch of frustration. The last thing she wanted to do right now was go downstairs and take the chance of running headlong into Karr.

"If it wasn't for the chain saw," she told the dog, "you'd still be asleep, and going outside would be the last thing on your mind. So could this at least wait till I've had my coffee?''

Tripp seemed to consider that for a moment, then started whining even louder. He was beginning to sound like the chain saw's twin, Maggie thought, and the last thing she needed was that sort of noise in stereo. She surrendered and got his leash.

The side door was propped open, and workers were hauling tools in from an enormous truck parked next to the house. Maggie had to wait while one crew maneuvered a long ladder around a corner and into the kitchen. She couldn't see what was going on there, but a moment later she heard the sharp crack of breaking glass and then a workman swearing. She wondered if it was a window or the glass front of one of the antique cabinets that was no more.

The swearing hadn't stopped yet when another man said, "The boss told us to gut the place, so what difference does it make?"

Maggie winced at the painfully vivid image.

"He told me the cabinets are already spoken for," the first man was saying as she went out the door. "So take it easy—somebody's going to pay a pretty penny for these."

If there's anything left of them, Maggie thought.

The sunlight was warm, but under the trees the air was still chilly. Tripp wanted to run, but Maggie refused to let him off the leash as she sometimes did. There was far too much going on. But after pulling him back a couple of times, to his obvious annoyance, she decided to compromise. If she jogged for a while, Tripp would get his exercise and maybe she'd work off some of her frustration.

She was deep into the woods, on the path that led to the lake, before she stopped for a breath. She sank down on a fallen tree to rest, and Tripp flung himself at her feet, panting.

Maggie tried to listen to the sounds of nature. The call of birds and the rustle of leaves always had the power to soothe her. But today, all she could hear was the chain saw. In fact, she could hear it every bit as clearly here as she had from her window this morning.

That, of course, was clearly impossible. She must be five hundred yards away. She sat up and listened, and realized that she was hearing a chorus of saws—for when one stopped, there was another, more distant one still assaulting the airwaves.

She closed her eyes and remembered the long, curving row of town houses Karr had built in Eagleton, with their pocket-size back gardens and tiny patches of grass in front. There was scarcely a tree in the whole row, and the few that did exist were mere saplings. If Karr was going to build in a similar pattern here, he'd have to clear-cut the heart of Eagle's Landing. From the sounds of it that was exactly what he was doing. And the work wasn't going to be finished anytime soon.

Maggie bit her lip. It was going to be extremely difficult to concentrate with all that noise going on. If Karr was intending to drive her out, he'd chosen a fiendishly effective way to start his campaign.

The walk to the house was considerably slower. Tripp padded along at her heels instead of darting ahead, and Maggie didn't even attempt to hurry him. She was no more eager to return to the melee than he was.

She wasn't surprised when she came around the last bend of the drive and saw a black Mercedes parked behind the house, but her heart started to beat a little faster in anticipation.

Karr was on the steps by the side entrance. He was wearing jeans and a dark green T-shirt—so he could help with the demolition, Maggie supposed. Just now he was supervising as the first white-painted kitchen cabinet was carried out and loaded into a truck. Once it was safely stowed, he put both hands on his hips, tipped his head to one side and surveyed Maggie.

She knew she must look a fright, warm and flushed from her run, with her hair starting to fall out of a careless ponytail. Nevertheless, there was something in the way he looked at her that made her feel tiny and very feminine.

But all he said was, "You don't exactly look like sunshine this morning. Did we wake you up too early?"

As if he understood the words, Tripp made a halfhearted dash at Karr and growled a little. But the dog's heart obviously wasn't in it, and finally he stopped growling and flopped at Maggie's feet, panting.

"And the toupee looks positively moth-eaten," Karr went on.

It was a temptation to let go of Tripp's leash and see what he'd do. Instead, Maggie tightened her grip and said coolly, "Oh, I'm fine. We're both quite happy, in fact. We've just been out for a good run."

"I see. You know, I can't figure out why you have a dog at all."

"Spend a lot of time worrying about it, do you?"

"Oh, no, it's just minor curiosity. If you had a big dog I could understand it, because he'd be protection. Or I could see you having a cat, for companionship. But to tie yourself down to an animal with the size and personality of a dust mop..."

"Do you often get bitten by dust mops?" She waved a hand toward the truck, where the men were loading a second cabinet. "I don't remember that door being broken last time I was in the kitchen."

"We had a little accident."

"That's too bad. Salvagers will pay a lot more if the glass is intact, I understand."

"Glass can be replaced."

"Maybe you should just wait a while till you can get some professional crews in here to do the work, instead of taking the chance of your guys damaging things."

"In about three weeks, I suppose you mean?"

Maggie smiled. "Isn't that amazing? You seem to have read my mind. I'll bet they'd work so much faster they'd make up the time, anyway. And if you ended up with less breakage, you'd be money ahead in the long run."

"I'll take my chances. I brought coffee out for the crew. Would you like some?"

Maggie shrugged, deliberately casual. "Might as well." There was no point in letting him guess how welcome a solid dose of caffeine would be right now—or that she felt like stirring aspirin into it instead of sugar.

There was not only a coffee urn set up on a folding table in the biggest drawing room, but a huge box of fresh doughnuts, as well. Tripp perked up at the aroma and sat down at her feet, head erect and one paw held out in a plea for her to share. Maggie broke off a bit of her glazed doughnut and dropped it to him.

"I meant what I told you last night, Karr," she said. "And psychological warfare is certainly not going to change my mind about suing you."

Karr poured coffee into foam cups and handed her one. "I don't have any idea what you're talking about."

"I mean all the noise and bustle you've created this morning for my benefit."

"For *your* benefit? Don't be ridiculous. I believe I told you once that I had crews impatiently waiting till they could start to work."

One of the workmen came in and picked up a doughnut. "Nice to see you again, ma'am."

"Again?" Karr asked.

Maggie said curtly, "We met—very briefly—at my window this morning."

"I see." A half-smile tugged at Karr's mouth. "No wonder everybody's been volunteering for chain saw duty," he mused.

Maggie longed to tip her coffee over his head.

"How long do you expect that oak to take?" Karr asked the workman.

"Most of the morning. That close to the house, we'll have to drop it branch by branch and lower each one with ropes."

"You're taking down the whole tree?" Maggie protested. "Look, I know the place is yours and you can do whatever you want, Karr, but—"

"Can I have that in writing? It's the first time you've actually admitted I have any rights at all."

Maggie glared at him. "But it would be a lot nicer development in the end if you left some of the big trees. And that's a great tree, so if you're only cutting it down to annoy me—"

Karr shook his head. "I don't know where you got the idea that annoying you is all I'm thinking about these days."

"Possibly because you do it so well," Maggie said under her breath.

"Perhaps you hadn't noticed how that tree blocked the afternoon light in your apartment. I'm actually doing you a favor—"

"Surely you don't expect me to believe that."

"Well, no, since you aren't going to be there long enough to enjoy it. I'm cutting the tree because it's dangerous."

"It's stood there for a hundred years!"

"Precisely. And it's dying, and half the trunk is hollow. I can't risk having men working around it in its present condition. Besides, it's in the way." He drained his cup and added, "And as long as we're on the subject, you're in the way, as well. May I remind you that your deadline is past, and you're now trespassing not only on my property but on my good nature?''

"What good nature? I tried to work out a compromise that would save us both a great deal of discomfort, and you aren't even reasonable enough to discuss it." Maggie put her chin up. "So go ahead and try to evict me. My lawyer is just waiting for the papers."

"Maybe I won't bother with papers."

She took one more sip and set her cup aside. "That is an empty threat." She wrapped Tripp's leash around her wrist and headed for the stairs. "Thanks for the coffee. It was certainly more pleasant than the conversation."

She knew Karr watched her till she was out of sight.

It was difficult to settle down to her work. Even with the windows closed, Maggie could hear every change in pitch of the chain saw. Finally, thinking they must be nearly finished, she took a break and went to check the crew's progress. In two hours the workmen had managed to remove only the smaller, leafy branches. A pitiful skeleton remained, stark and ghostly as an Oriental drawing. She could see hollow spots here and there in the trunk, spots that had been hidden by the leaves, and it annoyed her to have to admit that Karr had been right about that, too. It was lucky a windstorm hadn't blown the tree over against the house. It could have broken out half a dozen windows or even cracked the wall.

She left the windows open—it was impossible to shut the noise out anyway, and she hated to be cheated of the fresh air—and went to take a shower.

She'd hoped when the other tenants moved out that the water pressure might improve. It ought to have, she thought, without multiple demands on the system. But the water seemed to run at an even more leisurely pace than usual, and it took forever to rinse the shampoo from her hair. The lack of water pressure was the only thing she'd ever really disliked about living at Eagle's Landing, and this morning it was an irritation past all bearing. A really hot, hard shower might get rid of her headache, but this sad trickle didn't deserve the name.

She wasn't really sure just when she got the notion of doing something about it. It was just *there*, one of those perfect ideas that seem to spring full-fledged from out of the blue, and she didn't even bother to think it over. As soon as she was dry she wrapped herself in a terry robe and went to the telephone.

There were six plumbers in the vicinity of Eagleton, and she briefly considered soliciting bids from them all for a new water system for the whole of Eagle's Landing. It ought to get Elliot the Great to sit up and take notice, she thought, if he was interrupted by half a dozen plumbers one after another, all wanting his attention and his business.

No, that would be going too far. Still, she had to call four of the firms before she found someone who was free to come that morning and take a look at the unsatisfactory pipes.

"Grand," Maggie told him. "Take a good look around, and make sure you give the estimate to Karr Elliot." And, suddenly feeling in a much better mood, she dried her hair and went back to work. Even the whine of the chain saw wasn't nearly so annoying any more— or perhaps she was just growing slightly deaf from the roar.

She'd gotten so absorbed in the story she was writing that she'd entirely forgotten both time and plumbers, and even the sound of boots on the landing outside her apartment didn't warn her till Karr flung the door open and strode in.

Maggie sat up straight and tried to blink away her eyestrain. "What do you think you're doing? You can't come in here without knocking!"

"Try me," he growled. "Do you know anything about someone calling for a plumber, Rawlings?"

She bit her lip and for the first time noticed a man behind him, a big man wearing stained yellow coveralls and carrying an enormous toolbox. There were also a couple of Karr's workmen on the landing, she noted.

"Well," she said cautiously, "I did mention the water pressure to you. Several times, in fact. You didn't seem inclined to do anything about it, so—yes, I took it upon myself..." Her voice trailed off.

His eyes were the color of stainless steel, and there wasn't a trace of the dancing mischief she'd seen there so often.

He looked at her for a long moment, and then said levelly, "That does it."

Maggie was fascinated. Though his teeth were clenched, every word still sounded separate and distinct.

"You're going, Rawlings. Right now. There's an apartment set aside for you."

"In that complex of yours? It looks like a prison block!"

"I don't care what you think it looks like. You don't have to look at it at all if you don't want to. As far as I'm concerned, you can stay indoors the whole four weeks—or eight or sixteen or however long it turns out to be."

Maggie said sweetly, "Does this mean the offer to move in with you isn't good any more?"

Karr ignored her and called over his shoulder, "Riley and Evans, get some boxes up here on the double. Dump tools out of them if you have to." He grabbed Maggie's briefcase and started stuffing handfuls of manuscripts into the pockets.

Maggie shrieked, seized the strap and began pulling the papers out. It was a losing battle, because Karr obviously didn't care whether things were wrinkled or torn. By the time the briefcase was overflowing, one of the workmen had returned with a box, and Karr used his forearm to sweep stacks of paper into it, heedless of how they landed.

"Those are valuable papers," she cried. "You can't just throw them into a greasy box!"

"Watch me," Karr snapped.

"Dammit, you're not even supposed to be in here." She hardly knew what she was saying. She caught her computer by the corner as he started to sweep it into the box, and swung it out of his reach.

"Remember? Your lease says I can enter in an emergency. And baby, this is what I call an emergency. I assume, from all your talk about your work, that this is what you most need to take with you. The next thing I'm going to do is pack an overnight bag, just enough for you to get by—"

"This isn't funny anymore!"

"Who said I was joking?"

"You can't do this," Maggie said desperately. "It's not legal!" The chain saw had started up once more outside her window, and she had to shout to have any chance of being heard over the noise.

"Prove it."

"You'll be dealing with my attorney!"

"That's fine with me. By the time you can call him, the job will be done, and after that I don't care what happens."

The box was piled high by the time the table was bare, and Maggie looked at it in shock and disbelief. Her papers were stuffed in every which way. She'd never get any order to that mess again.

"I'm going to take this box downstairs," Karr said, "and I'll be right back. Don't lock the door or I'll kick it in. It is, after all, *my* door. In the meantime, if you don't want me rummaging through your undies, I'd suggest you start packing."

Maggie ran her hands through her hair. "You can't just throw me out with a box and an overnight bag. Wait till you hear what a court has to say about that!"

"I'm holding my breath in anticipation. Besides, I'm not impounding your stuff. We'll deliver it when we have time. You might be deciding where we're supposed to take it, though—does it go to the apartment complex or the dump?"

Maggie shrieked, "You—"

Karr didn't wait for the rest. Though the box was obviously heavy, he hefted it onto his shoulder and turned toward the door.

The plumber was still standing in the foyer, his mouth open. "Sorry," Maggie told him breathlessly. "It was a joke gone bad. Send me the bill for your time."

Karr said, "But don't bother to send it to Eagle's Landing, because she won't be here to get it!"

Maggie caught up with him at the top of the stairs. "Give me that," she demanded. "Those papers are mine, and I'm not going to let you out of my sight with them!"

He shrugged off her hand as easily as he'd dislodge a fly and started down. "Your treasures are safe with me. I haven't threatened to burn anything—yet."

Maggie made one more grab, but her hand closed on air. Thrown off balance by the motion, she felt her foot going out from under her. She reeled past Karr, clutching for him, for the rail, for the wall—and missed.

The fall seemed to last for the rest of her life as she rolled down the staircase—bumping, twisting, reaching out to protect her face, only to bang her hand against the edge of a step. She felt her leg twist and heard something snap. She tried to hold her head up, but she couldn't, and the thump as she hit the parquet floor of the stair landing sent her into blackness.

CHAPTER SEVEN

EVEN her eyelids hurt, and when Maggie managed to raise them, she saw that the staircase was revolving. So was Karr's face, which was bent closely over her. She shut her eyes again.

"Maggie." That husky voice had an edge to it that she'd never heard before. "Maggie, don't go away again. Hang on, sweetheart."

She blinked a little. Sweetheart? Where did he get off calling her that? It took nerve to practically push a woman down the steps and then call her sweetheart! And as for the way he was running his hands over her body... He didn't seem to be enjoying it, though, any more than she was.

His probing fingers hit a sore spot below her knee, and she jerked away from him, causing a new wave of pain to wash over her. "Would you lay off, Elliot?" she said feebly, and tried to uncurl herself from the tight little knot she'd ended up in. But she could only groan.

"What hurts?"

She wet her lips. "Everything."

"Don't try to move. Just lie still a minute, till we can sort out what works and what doesn't." He cupped his hands and massaged the length of her left arm, then carefully straightened it.

Maggie closed her eyes again. She was dizzy, but she didn't know whether that was from the bump to her head or the general pain level. She did know, however, that the sensation of Karr's hands pressing against her body was not helping matters. Not that his touch hurt, precisely—or at least it didn't most of the time.

"My hand hurts," she grumbled, and held it up.

"Can you move your fingers?"

She wriggled them obediently and tried to look at him again. This time nothing was revolving, but she could see a blizzard of white around her. She turned her head a little and regarded the mess. There were papers scattered down the stairs and across the landing. The box he'd been carrying was upside down on the bottom step. "Dammit, Elliot, I told you to be careful with that box," she said spitefully.

Karr didn't answer. "Your hand's okay, Maggie. I'm more worried about your leg."

"Oh, just help me up. I'll be fine once I get my breath back. And I'll be even better as soon as you've picked up all my stuff." She managed to roll onto her side and tried to raise herself up on her hands. The one she'd cracked against the stairs ached like fury, but she thought it would hold her weight.

Karr pushed her gently to the floor. "Nope," he said. "At a minimum, you've wrenched your knee, and it needs attention. Put your arms around my neck."

"If you think you get a hug for this—"

He gathered her up bodily, cradling her in his arms. "Pick up all this paper," he ordered one of the workmen. "I don't want to slip on it and drop her down another flight of steps."

"That's what you say," Maggie grumbled. "I wouldn't put it past you, myself. You'd do anything to get me out of here, wouldn't you, Karr?" She knew even as she said it how unfair it was, but the shock had dislodged her tongue somehow and she couldn't seem to get it under control. "How long was I out, anyway?"

She thought he wasn't going to answer, but finally he said quietly, "The longest twenty seconds of my life."

"Thought you'd killed me, hmm?" But the tone of his voice had reassured her, in an odd sort of way. Maggie put her head against his shoulder and sighed. Being carried like this really wasn't bad at all. She felt as light as a feather.

His grip tightened a little, and his breath stirred the hair at her temple. "Maggie, I'm sorry I lost my temper."

She perked up at that and opened her eyes. "Sorry enough to let me stay, I hope."

"Rawlings, you're incorrigible."

"Well, you *can't* kick me out now," she argued. "I'm wounded. If I'm too stiff even to move myself around, how can you expect me to pack up everything I own? And after what you did to that box, you can't believe I'll let you touch anything more."

He didn't even bother to answer that. *Two points for me*, Maggie thought.

The leather seat of the Mercedes didn't feel as soft as she remembered it, and she howled when he put her down.

"What is it?" Karr said.

"I must have bumped my hip, too." Maggie tried rubbing the sore spot, but her hand hurt too much. She gave it up as impossible.

She half-expected that the moment he'd handed her over to the emergency room personnel, he'd be history. But periodically through the next hour, while she was poked and prodded and X-rayed, Karr would appear at the door of the treatment room, looking concerned.

No doubt he was worried about the way this little episode would look to a judge, Maggie thought.

She finally told him to stop standing around in the hall because he was making her nervous. She didn't really intend it as an invitation to make himself at home, but he obviously did. He was sitting next to her bed when the doctor came in to tell her the only major damage was that she'd fractured one of the bones in her lower leg.

Maggie looked at the doctor in disbelief. "You've got to be kidding. That's the spot that hurts least!"

"You're quite lucky as it is, Miss Rawlings," the doctor said firmly. "With the fall you took, it could easily have been a compound fracture that would have required surgery. Or you could have a severe concussion, or a broken hip. Beside those possibilities, six weeks in a leg cast will be—"

"Six weeks?" Maggie howled. "I have to hobble around in a cast for *six weeks*?"

"Well, if you want to be technical," the doctor said, "it won't be the kind of cast you can put your weight on, so you won't be hobbling, exactly. You'll be using crutches. Don't worry, our physical therapists will come in tomorrow to teach you how to use them." He smiled cheerfully and departed to arrange for the cast to be applied.

"What did he mean, *tomorrow*?" Maggie asked warily.

"They'll no doubt want to keep you overnight for observation, just to be sure everything's all right."

"Oh, that's just great. You put them up to this, didn't you, Elliot?"

"Why would I—" Karr began, and abruptly stopped, as if he remembered all too clearly why he'd like to have her safely out of the way.

Maggie smiled grimly. "I know—you'd rather not admit it."

"I didn't organize this, Maggie." He stood up as an aide bustled in with a cart, and before Maggie could say another word, he was gone.

Not for long, however. As soon as she was settled in a room with her cast propped on a pillow, he reappeared. "I'll leave you to rest, and I'll pick you up

tomorrow when you're released. Do you want me to
bring you anything in the meantime? Or call anybody?
I've already talked to Libby, but is there anyone else?''

"No." Maggie tried to think. "There's nothing I can
think of...except Tripp. Oh, no, what am I going to do
about him? Maybe Libby will go get him—''

"I'll take care of the toupee.''

Maggie gave him a baleful look. "Is that offer supposed to comfort me?''

"Of course. As long as he behaves himself, I won't
deep fat fry him.'' He was gone before Maggie could
find an answer.

The cast weighed a ton, and it kept Maggie from sleeping.
Or perhaps it was her sore muscles that kept her awake.
Every time she moved she was reminded of her fall. And
when she did doze off, she recalled that helpless,
hopeless, weightless moment when she first knew she
was going down the stairs and nothing could stop her—
and instantly she'd jerk awake again.

As a result, she was heavy-eyed and in a particularly
glum mood the next morning. Breakfast was long over,
the doctor had given his approval for her to go home as
soon as the therapist had been in, and the nurse's aide
who helped her get dressed had slit the leg of her jeans
all the way to the hip to get them on over the cast.

Maggie was sitting in a chair with her foot propped
up on a hassock, gloomily surveying the cast and the
ruin of an expensive pair of jeans and waiting for Chad
Buckley to return her phone call, when a bubbly physical
therapist popped in.

"You're looking on top of the world today,'' the
therapist chirped.

"Personally, I think I look like a beached white
whale,'' Maggie muttered.

"Oh, you'll soon get used to the cast, and the six weeks will be gone before you know it. There are some tricks to using crutches, of course...."

"I hate to waste your time, but I used to play with crutches as a kid. It must be like riding a bike—you never forget how."

"You may find it a little different as an adult," the therapist warned. "Let me show you a few tricks."

Half an hour later she was still going strong. There was a knock on the half-open door, and Chad Buckley stuck his head in. His eyes widened in shock at the sight of her cast.

Maggie sank into her chair, relieved at the interruption. Every muscle ached, and she was ready to concede that it might take a while to get back into shape. "You got my message."

"I could hardly believe it when my secretary told me you were in the hospital. What did you do to yourself?"

The therapist said, "Would you like me to come back later, Miss Rawlings?"

"Oh—I think I've had enough for one session."

Chad started to back out of the room. "If you're busy—"

"Just finishing up." Maggie smiled at the therapist. "Thanks, I think I've got it now."

The therapist went out, and Maggie leaned back in her chair with a sigh of relief and smiled at Chad.

He grinned. "It's certainly nice to be so welcome. So how did you do all the damage?"

"I fell down a flight of stairs while in hot pursuit of my stolen property."

"I don't think I like the sound of this."

"Oh? I was sure you'd love it. It was my landlord who'd stolen the property."

"All right. It has some possibilities. Tell me more."

Maggie glanced at the clock. It was almost noon. Karr had said he'd pick her up this morning, but he hadn't shown up yet, and there was no predicting when he'd come. She supposed he might have said it only to keep her confined while he packed up the rest of her belongings.

"I'll be happy to tell you what happened," she said briskly. "But as long as you're here, would you spring me out of this place and take me home?"

Chad frowned. "Are you sure that's a good idea? Are you even allowed to leave, with that thing on?"

"Of course. Would I be dressed otherwise? I could be gone now if it wasn't for the therapist taking so long." Maggie pushed herself up from her chair and balanced on one foot while she fumbled with her crutches.

"Well—all right, if you're sure." He reached, a little awkwardly, for her elbow.

Maggie wondered what good he thought that kind of assistance would do. She shook her head at him and got the crutches properly centered under her arms.

Nothing to it, she thought. Once she had some practice...

Chad hovered all the way to the parking lot, so close that a couple of times Maggie almost bumped his foot with a crutch tip.

He was driving a little red sports car, and Maggie looked at it doubtfully. The seats were so low and the space around them so tiny that she wasn't certain she could fit her cast in at all. It took three tries and a bit of maneuvering before she was finally settled, and by then she was breathless with the effort.

"So what happened?" he asked as he started the engine.

"Elliot the Great and I had a little disagreement about whether I was moving out, and I fell down the stairs."

"You mean you fell, or he pushed you? We might be able to file charges for assault and battery, Margaret."

"No," Maggie said with regret. "He didn't shove me. In fact, I seem to recall that he tried to catch me. I reached for a box of papers he was carrying, but I missed and—boom."

"What papers?"

"All the stuff for the special issue I'm working on. Can I file charges on him for assaulting my property?"

"Not exactly."

Maggie went on, almost to herself, "I'll be a month sorting out the damage—except I haven't got a month. And if I don't get that special section done on time, I won't have a job, either."

"That fact might present some possibilities."

"Really? Take a left here and stay on this road all the way out of town."

They were on the outskirts of Eagleton before Chad asked, "Have you got a formal eviction notice yet?"

She shook her head. "Not unless it's posted on my door when I get home. He just walked in and started packing up my belongings."

"Now *that* gives me something to work with. I'll have to think it over, but I'll let you know what we can do."

Maggie said hesitantly, "Maybe I should warn you that I did a few things, too." She told him about the plumber.

Chad pursed his lips thoughtfully. "That doesn't help the case, Margaret. But I think in the end . . ." They were out in the country by then. He looked around and cast a speculative glance at Maggie. "Where are we going, anyway? Are you *sure* it's worth the kind of pitched battle we're talking about to stay out here in the back of beyond?"

"Eagle's Landing is very peaceful." At least it had been till yesterday, she reflected.

"So's a cemetery, but that doesn't mean it's a good place to live."

Maggie directed him to the side door, and as he came around the car to help her out, Chad cast a curious look at the house. "So this is what all the hubbub's about?"

Everything was quiet. She couldn't see the parking area at the back of the house, so she didn't know if the Mercedes was there. But not a single workman's van was in sight, and there wasn't a screeching chain saw to be heard anywhere. It was the lunch hour, Maggie noted. Maybe the workers had all gone off to have their break together.

She thought it more likely, however, that Karr had pulled them off the job—holding his troops in reserve, as it were, till she got home. After all, there was no sense in wasting all the noise and mess and dirt if the target of it wasn't there to be annoyed.

It was every bit as difficult to maneuver herself out of the sports car as it had been to get in. "Thanks for the ride, Chad."

"Sure you'll be all right? I wish I could stay a while and help you get settled, but I have appointments this afternoon." He smiled slyly. "I could bring dinner tonight, and come up with some ideas to take your mind off that leg—"

"If I'm feeling sociable I'll let you know," Maggie said hastily. "But I really think I'll need to catch up on my sleep."

He looked disappointed. "Well, I suppose you know best." He gave a cheerful wave, and the little red car zipped off down the drive.

Maggie swung up the side steps and managed to pull the door open. From the hall, she could see into the kitchen. All the cabinets were gone, and part of the ceiling had been ripped down. There was a ragged hole in one corner, where a cabinet must have resisted and been pulled loose by brute force. The destruction took her breath away.

She had to pick her way carefully across the parquet floor of the hallway to the stairs. The patterns in the wood were coated with sawdust, and debris was strewn everywhere. Even the tiniest bit of wood or dirt or broken glass could be hazardous to her crutches.

Besides, Maggie thought irritably, the floor ought to have a good sweeping before the workmen's feet ground the dirt and debris right through the finish and scarred the wood beyond repair—

But of course that hardly mattered, did it? It was one thing to remove kitchen cabinets or French doors or mantels, but it would be impractical to disassemble and try to save the delicate inlay of a parquet floor. It would take far too much time to be profitable—and so the bits of wood and dirt and broken glass would probably stay exactly where they were now.

She stopped at the bottom of the main stairs and took a deep breath. Never had the flight looked so long, so steep, so high. She balanced herself carefully on one foot, braced the crutches on the first step and levered herself up.

"One down, twenty-odd to go," she told herself. That was only this flight, of course. She wouldn't even think about the next set, leading to her apartment, till she got there. "Slow and steady, Maggie—that's the way."

Ever so slowly she climbed, eight inches at a time. Her arms were aching with the effort by the time she reached the next floor, and it was a relief to be back on flat territory for a few moments, till she got across the landing and to the attic stairs. They were narrower, and she had to be even more careful with the crutches. But finally she was at the top.

Beyond the closed door of her apartment, Tripp was yelping in excitement. "It's okay, baby," Maggie soothed. "It's just going to take me longer than usual to get around, I'm afraid. You'll have to be patient. I'll be there in a minute."

The door was locked. And, she remembered with dismay, her key was inside, safely tucked into her handbag.

After her fall, locking her apartment had been the farthest thing from her thoughts. But Karr had obviously remembered.

Of course, Maggie thought. He wouldn't want to be held responsible for any damage or loss while he was in charge. And she really couldn't blame him. She was the one who'd been threatening him with lawsuits right and left.

But how had he done it? Had he gone looking for her key? She hoped he'd found the one in her handbag and not the spare she'd long ago hidden on the landing in case of emergency.

Or had he perhaps changed the locks in order to keep her out? Surely not. He was planning to pick her up at the hospital himself, so he wouldn't expect her to be back yet.

Under normal circumstances, she had to stand on her tiptoes to reach the ledge where she'd stowed the extra key. Today, balancing on one foot, it was even more of a challenge. But the key was there, and to her relief, it fit the lock.

She let herself in and sank into the nearest chair, mopping perspiration from her brow. The therapist was right. This business of being on crutches *was* a lot more difficult than she remembered. It had seemed so much more an adventure when she was a child, playing with an old, discarded set.

Tripp was bouncing around her like a Ping-Pong ball, jumping up in an effort to lick her, even leaping onto her lap and then off again, too excited to stay still.

Maggie tried to pet him, but he was too impatient, so she sat back in her chair and tried to relax. She was half-afraid to look around.

But everything seemed just the same as she'd left it. Even her papers had been returned, she was surprised to see. The box sat squarely in the center of the library table. The contents were a mess, of course—the box looked as if her notes and files had been picked up at random from the stairs and thrust in any old way.

She sighed. It appeared she hadn't overestimated the effort of straightening them out. But she'd have nothing but work to occupy her time for the next few weeks—she certainly wasn't going to be doing any jogging.

She'd half expected to see all her things packed up, but apparently nothing had been touched. Perhaps Karr really was sorry for losing his temper, she thought. That possibility, coupled with the unarguable fact that he was partially responsible for her injury, probably put Maggie in the best bargaining position she'd occupied all along.

Tripp sat at her feet, bright eyes focused on her face, and gave his I-want-to-go-out bark.

"No," Maggie said firmly.

Tripp tipped his head to one side and repeated the demand.

Maggie groaned. There was no telling how long it had been since the dog had been walked. She didn't doubt that Karr had kept his word. After all, she hadn't forced him to volunteer his services as a dog sitter.

But what if Tripp had refused to have anything to do with him? The dog had a stubborn streak every inch as big as he was, and he cordially hated Elliot the Great. Why hadn't she thought of that yesterday, and insisted that Karr call Libby to take charge of the dog?

Because you weren't thinking straight, Maggie reminded herself. And so, when Libby had come to the hospital last night, Maggie had assured her there was nothing that needed doing.

Besides, she reminded herself, it was no big deal. She might as well get used to trekking up and down the stairs. She could hardly lock herself in the apartment for the next few weeks, so she might as well start right now by learning how to manage.

She got Tripp's leash and hooked it to his collar, but before she'd even reached the door he'd wrapped himself around her crutch. If he did that on the stairs, she'd go down again for sure. Maggie unhooked the leash and tied it around her waist.

The staircase looked steeper from the top, and the idea of going down was far more threatening than coming up had been. Tripp bounded halfway down and stopped to bark impatiently at her. Maggie balanced herself carefully and swallowed hard, and remembered what the therapist had said this morning about the proper way to tackle stairs.

She tried not to think about the last time she'd come down this flight of steps, out of control, bouncing, rolling and coming to rest with a broken bone. And that was with the use of both feet, and with both hands free....

Stop it, she told herself, and before she could psych herself out of making the effort, she took the first step.

By the time she got to the bottom, she was trembling with exertion and her skin was damp. But she'd made it, and the first time, she told herself, was much the hardest. She could do this.

She sat down on the bottom step, untied the leash from her waist and snapped it to Tripp's collar. He danced away, pulling the leash out of her hand. Maggie grabbed for it and missed, and the dog zoomed playfully down the hall and out of sight. She called him, without result, and irritably hauled herself upright once more to follow.

He was nowhere in sight, and the side door was standing half open. She must not have closed it firmly when she came in. Maggie was annoyed with herself, but not seriously concerned. There was no one around, and she sometimes let Tripp run in the grassy area just across the drive. Surely he'd stop there, delighted with his freedom.

She was at the door when she saw the dog dart across the drive and under the wheels of a black Mercedes.

She heard the sharp squeal of brakes and closed her eyes, but the sight was imprinted on her retinas. Tripp was so small, so fast, so hard to see. How could anyone avoid hitting him? And he was so tiny and fragile that if a tire had so much as grazed him...

She tried to run, for an instant forgetting the crutches that handicapped her. Her weak foot went out from under her, the crutches slipped, and she fell heavily against the side rail of the little porch.

A car door slammed, and Karr took the steps in a single leap, bellowing, "How the hell did that dog get loose?" He stopped when he saw Maggie clutching the rail and trying to regain her balance. "You. I ought to have known."

The words were tart, but his touch was firmly gentle as he slid an arm around her waist and lifted her upright, holding her till she was balanced on her good foot. "Hang onto the post for a second," he ordered, and retrieved her crutches.

"Is Tripp—" Maggie couldn't finish the sentence, and she couldn't bear to look at the driveway.

"He appeared to be fine when I last saw him," Karr said dryly. "He ran practically between the wheels, and the last glimpse I got, he was headed at top speed into the woods. A sensible choice, I must admit. If I'd had my hands on him at that moment I'd have made him into a fur scarf."

Sheer relief made Maggie snap, "Don't you think you came close enough to doing just that?"

"I was expecting him to be upstairs where he belongs," Karr pointed out.

Maggie bit her lip. That *had* been a fancy piece of driving. She had thought there was no way he could escape hitting the dog. She ought at least to tell him she appreciated his skill.

"Dammit, Maggie, what are you doing back here, anyway? I came to the hospital just as I said I would— but you weren't there, and nobody seemed to know where you'd gone."

The desire to apologize evaporated, and Maggie put her chin up. "I came home. Where did you think I'd go?"

"You're right. I ought to have known." He perched on the rail, arms folded across his chest, and added calmly, "I suppose you've been upstairs? But of course you must have been, to get the dog."

Maggie studied him warily, but he sounded as if he was merely making conversation. He didn't seem to be defensive, and for a wonder, he'd stopped issuing accusations, too.

Maybe they could talk about this in a civilized manner after all, she thought, and nodded.

"And how did you get along?" Karr asked politely. The question seemed to be no more than a superficial query about her health.

"Just fine." She kept her voice cool.

Karr slid off the rail and came over to her. Both Maggie's hands were occupied with the crutches, so she couldn't stop him from cupping her chin in one hand and raising her face to the light. "You're a liar, too," he said harshly. "You're absolutely gray with the effort." He released her abruptly. "Dammit, Maggie, don't you have any sense at all? What if you'd fallen again? You're shaking, and you look like hell—like you're going into shock."

"Of course I'm in shock. My dog's gone—"

"He'll come back. The toupee's not so dumb that he doesn't know a good thing when he sees one."

"But he's dragging a leash. He'll get hung up and strangle himself!" Maggie was trembling in earnest now.

To his credit, Karr didn't point out that it was Maggie's own fault that her dog was on the loose. He swore, under his breath, and put his arms around her, crutches and all.

Maggie leaned against him, grateful that for a moment or two she didn't have to think about her balance. He would keep her from falling. But within seconds she realized that it wasn't only support he was offering—his warmth was comforting, too. She hadn't realized how cold and clammy she felt, and how safe she was in his arms....

She nestled closer and burst into tears.

Karr's lips brushed her temple in a caress that wasn't quite a kiss, but wasn't an accident, either. The contact scorched Maggie all the way to her core.

"Look," he said finally, "I'll make you a deal, Maggie. I'll find your damned dog if you'll go somewhere that you'll be safe."

Maggie considered the offer and almost turned it down. He'd seize any excuse to get her out of Eagle's Landing. And surely he'd go looking for Tripp in any case—when she'd mentioned the leash, he'd looked just a little sick himself.

But the thought of tackling the stairs again left her cold. The lesson had been a hard one, but the fact was she didn't have stamina enough right now to manage the climb, and she wasn't going to regain it anytime soon. And if she couldn't go up and down with relative ease, without fearing every moment that she would fall again... Karr had hit a nerve with that mention of safety. What if there was a fire, and she couldn't get down the stairs in a hurry?

It broke her heart to admit it, but she simply couldn't manage Eagle's Landing under these conditions. So she might as well surrender gracefully—while Karr was still willing to provide her with a place to live. She'd have to look for something permanent, of course, as soon as she was fit again—but right now she simply had no alternative but to accept what he offered.

"All right," she mumbled. The words seemed to stick in her throat. "Whatever you say."

She had forgotten how beautiful his smile was, and how it seemed to light up his entire face. How long had it been since he'd smiled at her, anyway? A couple of days, she thought. She hadn't realized how much she had missed it.

She was still a bit bemused at the effect a simple smile could have on her as Karr settled her in the Mercedes and got behind the wheel.

"Aren't you going to look for Tripp?" she protested. "I'll be fine right here in the meantime."

Karr shook his head. "I'm going to give him a chance to wear himself out first. Once he stops running he'll be a great deal easier to find."

"But what if he—"

"Maggie, you're going. Now."

There was no arguing with the steel thread in his voice. He had sounded just like this yesterday as he issued his ultimatum. But even though she knew it would be prudent to back off, Maggie heard herself saying, "What's the matter? Don't you trust me to keep my part of the bargain?"

His eyebrows rose very slightly. "Do you really want me to answer that?"

She didn't. "So where do you suggest I go?"

"Well, that's a problem. When I mentioned the apartment yesterday, I forgot that the tenants' association has voted not to allow pets."

"I haven't got one any more," Maggie pointed out drearily.

"You will have. I'll find the little mutt if it takes all week—I promise."

Maggie would have thanked him for the determination, but she was afraid she'd cry if she tried. "The condos, then?"

Karr shook his head. "I checked this morning, but there are only second-floor units left."

"Then what?" She wasn't even thinking about the question—her mind was still on Tripp. "Your town house has stairs, too, doesn't it?"

He shot a look at her, and the warmth in his gaze seemed to set her blood on fire. "Been giving some thought to that offer, have you?" he asked lazily. "Is that why you didn't stop by that afternoon—because you were scared you'd end up staying?"

Maggie glared at him, annoyed at herself for letting that bedroom voice of his conjure up all kinds of exciting, unexplainable sensations. Why *had* that comment popped into her mind—and at such an inconvenient time? "You're a dreamer, Elliot."

Karr laughed. "And here I thought you weren't taking my offer seriously."

"I'm not. So where are you taking me? Libby has stairs, too."

"And she starts to work next week. You shouldn't be alone."

That was obvious. If she couldn't carry something like Tripp's leash, how was she going to manage a plate or a book? But what were the options? There was no one she could ask for such a favor.

They were well into Eagleton by then, in a neighborhood of large houses—mansions, really, set far apart
and well back from a tree-lined boulevard across from
a manicured park.

"This is gorgeous," she breathed.

"Haven't you been here before? It's one of the oldest
neighborhoods, where the families who started the town
all gathered together. It's still called Society Flats,
sometimes."

The house he took her to was smaller than many of
the others. A neatly kept brick Georgian, it had a cir-
cular drive and a huge old maple tree, which gracefully
framed the front entrance.

"Do I know who lives here?" Maggie asked uncer-
tainly as the Mercedes pulled up to the front door.

"Not yet." Karr came around to help her out. "I've
found you a private-duty registered nurse who's agreed
to take you into her home till you're healed."

Maggie refused to move. "Karr, don't you think that's
overkill? Having someone around to give me a hand is
one thing, but I don't need a full-time nurse, for heaven's
sake. And I certainly can't afford—"

He didn't seem to hear her. "By the way, she's also
my mother." Sliding one arm under her knees and the
other around her back, he lifted Maggie out of the car.
"And I'm rather fond of her. So you'll treat her more
gently than you do me—won't you, darling?"

CHAPTER EIGHT

"Your mother?" Maggie wriggled a little, but to no avail. Karr held her easily well off the ground. "Why's your mother taking in private patients?"

"Well, not because she couldn't find a job in a hospital somewhere. I assure you she's an extremely competent nurse. But of course you can ask to see her diploma if you're not convinced of her skills."

"Don't be ridiculous. You know perfectly well that isn't what I meant. It can't be for the money, that's all, or she wouldn't be living in this kind of neighborhood. So why would she bother with—"

"Well, you never know," Karr said thoughtfully. "You're right, this is an expensive neighborhood. So I suppose she might be having trouble making ends meet, and since I'm far too self-centered to help her out..."

Maggie would have kicked him if she'd had full use of her body. "That's the stupidest thing I've heard you say all week."

"You don't think I'm cheap and selfish? My goodness, that *is* progress."

At the range of six inches, his smile was even more devastating. Maggie felt a little dizzy, and it took effort to keep her voice level. "At least not where your mother's concerned. But don't get a big head over my approval— I know perfectly well the only reason you're treating me decently at the moment is that I could sue you for my fall."

"Now wait a minute. How are you planning to shift the blame to me?"

"Illegal eviction," Maggie said briefly. "And my attorney agrees. Now will you at least put me down and give me my crutches so I can walk in like a lady, under my own power?"

"Tell the truth—you're afraid if you keep talking to me like that, I'll drop you." Karr set her carefully on her one good foot and slid both hands to her waist to steady her.

"No, I figured the alternative was that you'd throw me over your shoulder and haul me in like a sack of potatoes."

He grinned. "What a gracious capitulation!"

The front door opened, and a tall, slender woman with soft gray hair looked out.

Oh, great, Maggie thought. From Mrs. Elliot's point of view, it must look as if her son's arms were around Maggie for a great deal more reason than mere physical support.

But Karr didn't seem to notice. He stood there for a long moment looking at her, and then helped her balance against the Mercedes while he got her crutches.

The walk to the house looked immensely long. The stairs at Eagle's Landing had robbed Maggie of more energy than she'd expected, and she couldn't quite suppress a sigh. Before she realized what he intended, Karr had set the crutches aside and picked her up once more.

"Put me down," she demanded, but it was a half-hearted protest, and Karr ignored her.

He swept her across the threshold, leaned down to kiss his mother's cheek and said, "Where do you want me to drop the baggage?"

"On the couch, I think." Mrs. Elliot's tone was almost businesslike, but her voice held some of the same soft huskiness that made Karr's so distinctive. "We'll start getting acquainted, if you're not too exhausted, Maggie."

"Well, I like that." Karr sounded aggrieved. "I carry you in, but Mom's worried about whether *you're* exhausted."

Maggie summoned a rather shaky smile. "I really appreciate this, Mrs. Elliot."

"It's nothing, my dear. And I'm Brenda, please." She studied Maggie's face and turned to Karr. "I thought you were bringing her straight from the hospital, but she looks a little gray. Have you let her wear herself out?"

"Let her? I'd like to see anyone stop her," Karr complained. He strode across the marble-floored central hall to a big living room and set Maggie gently down on a luxuriously long couch. "But that figures—she acts like a fool, and I get the blame."

Brenda paid no attention to his protest. "I baked your favorite cookies, Karr. Can you stay a while?"

He shook his head. "Sorry to kiss and run, Mom, but I have to go rescue a toupee from his fate."

Brenda blinked once, as if she wasn't sure she was hearing correctly. But she didn't ask for an explanation, Maggie noted.

She waited at the front door till Karr brought Maggie's crutches, and then came into the living room.

"He means he's going to look for my dog," Maggie explained.

"Well, that's a comfort. With Karr, you never quite know." Brenda pulled up a hassock and perched on the corner of it, studying Maggie's face and the pristine white cast that stretched from her toes to well above her knee. "The orthopedics people had a good time with you, didn't they? No one ever answered my question, you know. *Have* you done something foolish to wear yourself out this morning, or are you feeling generally awful?"

Maggie bit her lip. "I was foolish," she admitted.

"Well, that's good."

"It is?"

"Of course. If you've overdone things, a rest should take care of it. If there wasn't a good reason for the way you look at the moment, I'd be far more concerned." She stood up. "May I get you a soft drink or a cup of tea?"

"Oh, please, don't wait on me. I'm not used to it—"

Brenda Elliot smiled, and suddenly she looked very much like Karr. The resemblance took Maggie's breath away.

"I don't plan to," Brenda said gently. "But just now you need a rest. So how about some tea and a good chat? If we're going to be housemates for a month or so, the sooner we get to know each other the better."

Until the comfort of Brenda's words washed over her, Maggie hadn't realized how tense she'd become. She couldn't remember the last time she'd been able to simply relax and let someone take care of her. "That would be lovely," she said simply, and leaned back, letting the peaceful quiet of the room wash over her. She could almost feel each muscle slowly loosening as the tension drained away. "Do you take in patients often?"

"Oh, no. You're my first in years—but Karr says you're extremely special. I'll be back in just a minute."

Extremely special?

Maggie could hear him saying it, his husky voice edged with irony, and her anxiety reappeared in a flood. It was just as well Brenda hadn't waited for an answer, Maggie thought. She hadn't a clue what to say.

Brenda Elliot had not only a dry sense of humor, which Maggie quickly came to appreciate, but a finely tuned perception where her patient was involved. She seemed able to detect Maggie's aches even before Maggie herself was fully aware of them.

"Time for a painkiller and a nap," she decreed after their cup of tea, and showed Maggie to a pleasant ground-floor bedroom at the back of the house. "We remodeled this room and added the bath when Karr's grandmother—my mother-in-law—couldn't live alone any more. These days I use it mostly as an office, but I've moved my things out so you'll have room to work. Is Karr bringing your things over?"

"I don't know. I didn't think to ask him."

Brenda tucked a soft knitted blanket over her. "Well, don't worry about it. Perhaps later you can make out a list of what you'll need, and I'll go out. We certainly can't have you taking chances on the stairs at Eagle's Landing—they're frightful."

Maggie wasn't about to admit that was exactly what she'd done. "You know the house?"

"I've been in it. Before it was converted to apartments, the last family who lived there threw it open for a tour to raise funds for the local historical society."

"I didn't know we had one."

"Oh, yes. It's very small, and not very active—I'm afraid I'm just about the youngest member."

It would have made for some dark humor, Maggie thought, if during her abortive drive to save Eagle's Landing she'd tracked down the local historical society, called to complain about Elliot the Great and ended up talking to his mother!

After Brenda left, Maggie settled back against the pillows and looked around. Brenda had drawn the curtains, but enough afternoon light seeped through the panels to let her study the room. She thought it must have been a music room when the house was new, or perhaps a study, for it was set slightly apart from the rest of the house as if to isolate sound. The room was nicely proportioned, with a high ceiling set off by a deep, intricately carved crown molding. The floor was random-width oak boards, with no rugs to create a hazard for her crutches. The desk was big and practical, the bath small but efficient.

If she couldn't be at home, this was by far the best choice open to her. It was only now beginning to sink in on Maggie how terribly difficult it would have been to manage on her own—and how few options she'd had. For someone as sensitive of her privacy as Maggie was, having just anyone around wasn't the answer. The idea of someone constantly hovering over her was distasteful—but if she had to ask for each tiny bit of help, that would perhaps be even worse.

But Brenda Elliot seemed to have a gift for helping without smothering. Maggie genuinely liked the woman and sensed that spending a month in her company would be no effort at all.

Now if Karr had only found Tripp, safe and unhurt, her cup would be full to overflowing....

She dozed off still thinking of the dog and woke with a jolt, not sure where she was and completely confused about the time. Did the soft light that filtered through the curtains, casting long shadows across the floor, mean it was early evening or early morning?

Evening, she realized. She'd napped for several hours, but she hadn't slept around the clock as she'd feared. She washed her face and straightened her rumpled blouse as best she could. When Brenda went out to get things from her apartment, Maggie decided, clothes would be just as high on the priority list as her computer was.

As Maggie came slowly into the living room, Brenda put down the current issue of *Today's Woman* and looked up with a smile. "You have your color back," she observed. "That's good. How's your appetite? I've got a chicken dish simmering for dinner."

"It sounds wonderful—I'm hungry." Maggie looked around, hoping against hope to see a tiny, enthusiastic

Yorkie. But of course, if Tripp had been in the room, he'd have greeted her instantly. "Has Karr been back?"

Brenda shook her head. "I'm afraid not. Dinner won't be ready for a while, but I'll get you a snack in the meantime."

Before Maggie could protest at the extra bother, Brenda went off down the center hall toward the kitchen.

Maggie sat down on the couch and stared at the fire, which blazed cheerfully on the hearth. She shouldn't have pinned her hopes on Karr finding the dog, she supposed. Even though he'd said he'd search for Tripp...

A nasty little voice in the back of her mind whispered that Karr had other things to do, things that were certainly more important to him than hunting for her dog. Maybe he'd only said he'd look in order to get her into the Mercedes and away from Eagle's Landing. He didn't even *like* the animal....

Maggie smothered the doubt as firmly as she'd have stepped on a bug. Of course Karr had hunted, she told herself. He wouldn't have told her he'd look if he didn't intend to—so if Karr hadn't found Tripp, it was because the dog was simply gone.

A cold little ache settled around her heart as she realized that she might never know exactly what had happened to her pet.

Deliberately, she picked up the magazine Brenda had tossed aside and tried to concentrate on it. She'd glanced at the issue a couple of weeks ago, as soon as it had come off the press, just to be sure that the printers hadn't made any horrible errors and the features she'd worked on had turned out as she'd expected.

But even though there was seldom time in her busy schedule to really enjoy the fruits of her work, the magazine couldn't hold her attention. She laid it aside and started toward the kitchen. Perhaps she could help with dinner, and keeping her hands busy might help her stop thinking of Tripp.

The doorbell rang just as she passed through the hall, startling her so that her crutch skidded slightly on the marble floor. She didn't wait for Brenda to come around the corner but pulled the door open.

Karr stood on the step, wearing a bulky jacket zipped halfway up. The breeze was crisper than it had been earlier in the day, and Maggie shivered a little—partly from the cold air, and partly because his hands were empty. He wasn't holding a leash, and that meant she wasn't going to get her dog back.

Her eyes filled with tears. Tripp had been her companion since she'd moved into Eagle's Landing. He was the first pet she'd ever had—and life would be very lonely without him.

The front of Karr's jacket seemed to move, but Maggie thought it was simply because her eyes were blurry. Then a beady-eyed little face poked out above the zipper.

"Tripp!" Maggie shrieked, and dropped a crutch to reach for him.

Karr took a quick step and put his arm around her. "Watch out—I guarantee you don't want to take a fall on this marble."

Maggie hardly heard him. The Yorkie stretched up to lick her face. He looked as if he was grinning.

"Where did you find him?" she demanded. There was a catch in her voice, which hurt her throat. "It's been so long, I thought he was gone for sure."

"Now that's enough to make me feel insulted," Karr complained. "Didn't you have faith in me? I told you I'd find the dust mop."

"Toupee," she corrected, and tried to blink the tears away. "I can't believe he's letting you carry him like that."

"I'm not so sure he likes it, but his fur's still damp, so I thought I'd better keep him out of the wind."

"Damp? Where was he?"

"Down by the lake. That's what held us up. He was so coated with mud I wasn't sure which end was which, and I knew Mother would have a fit if I brought him in that condition, so I gave him a bath."

"A *what*?"

Karr's eyebrows rose. "You disapprove of baths?"

"Tripp hates getting wet. I can hardly hold him down long enough to get him clean."

"That's because he's got you wrapped around his paw. Once he realized I meant business, he settled right down." Karr unzipped the jacket and, keeping one arm around Maggie's waist to steady her, set the dog on the floor.

Tripp danced a little as his paws hit the cold marble, and with an eye to comfort he headed straight for the carpeted living room and flopped down in front of the fire.

With a smile, Maggie watched him making himself at home. "Thanks for finding him, Karr," she said softly. "I know he's been an awful nuisance, but he's very special to me."

"You both have your moments." Karr's voice was gruff, and she looked at him in surprise.

She'd been too preoccupied with the dog to notice how very close Karr was standing. But then, he was practically holding her up. His arm was like a steel band, strong and impersonal, making it as safe to lean on him as on a rock....

And she was leaning. The entire length of her body was pressed against him, and his warmth had soaked straight through her clothes, spreading till every inch of her skin seemed to be aflame from the contact. And his eyes... She met his gaze, dark and intense and far from impersonal, and suddenly she had to make an effort to breathe.

He was going to kiss her, and Maggie didn't mind at all. The realization hit her hard. Surely she *ought* to mind. But at the moment she couldn't quite remember why.

The first brush of his lips against hers made her head swim, and she clutched at him in something close to desperation, afraid that if she didn't hold on as tightly as she could, she would spin dizzily into perpetual darkness. He tasted of coffee, and his cologne mixed nicely with the scent of soap. The combination made her senses reel, and she pressed herself even closer, knowing that the solidness of him was her link with reality.

As if from a great distance, she heard a bang, and Karr raised his head. "There went the other crutch," he said, with a tiny chuckle in his voice.

Dimly, Maggie realized that she had planted both hands against his chest and twisted the front of his jacket into makeshift handles. No wonder he was amused! She tried to push herself away and smooth out the wrinkles she'd made in his jacket, but Karr's hands remained steady on her hips.

"That was a very pleasant thank-you, Maggie, my dear."

She could feel color washing over her face. He sounded as if she'd written him a pleasant little note, not kissed him as if he was her life's breath.

And that was just as well, she told herself grimly. However nice he was being this afternoon, she'd better not allow herself to forget that Karr had his own agenda.

"And that wasn't a bad try at convincing me not to sue you, either," she murmured. "Of course, it didn't accomplish the purpose, but still—" From the corner of her eye, she caught a flash of movement at the back of

the hall, and moaned. "Oh, no. Your mother saw that."
She braced herself, expecting him to pull away.

But he didn't. "No doubt," he said comfortably.

"Don't you mind?"

"Well, I'm grown up now, and I figure I can kiss
whomever I want, whether or not my mother's watching.
Besides, that little scene should go a long way toward
convincing her that I'm attracted to you."

Maggie was startled. He sounded almost casual about
it—even slightly amused at the idea. "What? You can't
possibly want her to think that you and I—" She
swallowed hard. "That's insane, Karr. What are you
thinking of?"

Karr shrugged. "Well, I had to give her some reason
she should take you in. I could hardly tell her you're the
bane of my existence, could I? Or that you're threatening to drag me into court? She'd have told me to stash
you in a rooming house somewhere." He studied her
critically. "I think you've been standing too long,
Maggie. You've got hardly any color left." He scooped
her up in his arms. "Where were you going, anyway?"

"I can get there on my own power," Maggie an-
nounced. "This caveman act of yours is getting to be a
nasty habit, Karr."

He shrugged. "Really? What are you planning to do
about it?"

From behind them, Brenda said calmly, "I'm glad
you're back, Karr. Dinner will be ready in an hour—can
you stay and entertain Maggie?"

His eyes brightened, and his voice was husky. "I'll do
my very best."

Maggie wanted to bury her head, but since the only
hiding spot within reach was Karr's shoulder, she thought
a pretense of dignity was a better choice. What other
options did she have, after all, when she was bundled
up in his arms, four feet off the floor?

Brenda set the tray she was carrying on the coffee table. Tripp looked up at her speculatively, decided that the aromas from the tray made Brenda a friend and sat up to beg.

Karr put Maggie on the love seat nearest the fire and slid the hassock neatly under her cast. "Well, I like that," he told the dog. "What an apple-polisher you are!" Before Maggie could ask him to retrieve her crutches from the hall, he sat down next to her, rather closer than she felt was comfortable, reached for a cracker and a bit of cheese from the tray and popped the combination into his mouth whole.

Tripp watched him mournfully and stood beside the couch, bracing his front paws on Karr's knee.

"Down," Maggie ordered, and turned to Brenda. "I didn't think to ask about the dog, but if you don't want him around—" She racked her brain for another possibility, and turned to Karr, her eyes pleading.

"Don't look at me," he said lazily. "I've done my bit just by finding him. I'm not adopting him. And who says Mother doesn't like dogs, anyway? I just said she doesn't care for muddy ones."

"Dogs are certainly better than tarantulas." Brenda handed Maggie a glass of white wine. "Or, for that matter, the baby raccoon you insisted on keeping."

"You had tarantulas?" Maggie asked.

Karr ate another chunk of cheese. "Why do women object to spiders, anyway? They were certainly less trouble than the raccoon. He chewed a hole in a kitchen cabinet one night, and it took a whole month of my allowance to repair the damage."

"The tarantulas, on the other hand, cost me the best housekeeper I ever had," Brenda said calmly. "Have some cheese, Maggie, before Karr consumes it all."

Karr propped an elbow on the back of the love seat and leaned toward Maggie. "You're a troublemaker, you know that?"

"*Me?*"

"Yes. Mother hadn't mentioned the tarantulas getting loose in almost five years. Then you come along, and—"

"And that makes it my fault?" Maggie half-turned to face him, and the brilliance of his smile almost stunned her.

Thank heaven he'd warned her this whole thing was only a bit of playacting. She hated to think what craziness would be running through her mind right now if she thought he might be serious.

But playacting or not, Maggie decided, she'd have to get him alone very soon and put a stop to this. It was nothing but a silly trick, anyway.

And also not a very flattering one, when she stopped to think about it. He seemed to be implying that Brenda couldn't possibly like Maggie enough to take her in for her own sake. That insult must be why she had such an odd, empty feeling in the pit of her stomach.

But in the meantime, all she could do was be a good sport about it. She reached for her wineglass, and Tripp stretched out his tongue and lazily lapped at her wrist.

She stared at the dog in amazement. When had he crept into Karr's lap and curled up? "What have you done to my dog?" she demanded. "He's behaving as if you've brainwashed him."

Karr gave her a disbelieving look. "Why would I want him to worship me? He's a damned nuisance."

"Well, something changed his attitude about you."

"Oh, that's easily explained. I found him stranded in a brier patch, and before I started cutting him out, we had a little man-to-toupee chat about his behavior." Tripp yawned and rolled over in Karr's lap to display a sensitive patch of tummy. "I thought we'd got a few things straightened out, but I may have gone a bit too far." Karr stroked the soft fur.

Maggie shook her head in disbelief.

"Your box of papers is in the Mercedes, by the way," Karr went on. "And your computer. Don't let me forget to bring it in. I've made arrangements for Libby to pack your clothes and everything you'll need for a while. Let her know what you want, and she'll make sure it gets here."

"But she's got so many other things to do, Karr. Between moving and unpacking and starting to work—"

He shrugged. "I'll just make that her first assignment. What do you suggest instead? You can't do it, and though Mom doesn't realize it yet, she'll have her hands full keeping you under control."

Maggie was quiet. If only she could get up those stairs . . . But she couldn't, and the box of papers was a painful reminder that even if she was physically able to get to her apartment, she didn't have time to deal with the details. She'd lost two more days because of this accident, and the deadline was creeping closer.

Karr stretched an arm across the back of the couch, around her shoulders, and murmured, "Unless, of course, you'd like me to do it myself."

Maggie turned her head abruptly. He'd moved so close that his lips brushed her temple. The contact was like an electrical charge surging through her, but it didn't seem to affect Karr at all. He gave her a slow, sultry smile, and his fingertips started to draw slow, hypnotic circles on her upper arm. It was the first time Maggie had ever suspected that particular spot could be a sensual zone.

The man was incorrigible. It was clear that the sooner she put a stop to all this the better off she'd be.

And she'd do exactly that, she told herself. But not right now.

The next morning Libby stopped by with a suitcase. "I figured you'd want mostly casual things," she said. "But I couldn't find much. Do you realize how few of your clothes will fit over a cast?"

Maggie sighed. "I suppose I'll have to buy a whole new wardrobe. Of course, I could just charge it to Karr. He owes me." She recalled, a second too late, that Brenda was in the room, and shot a glance at her.

"He'd probably pay it," Brenda said calmly, and went on unpacking the suitcase, laying sweat suits neatly in drawers. "Ever since he called you one night while he was here, I've been dying to meet you."

So it was his mother he'd been sharing that steak with.

"I've never heard Karr sound as he does when he talks to you, Maggie."

Libby asked brightly, "Oh, really?"

"Yes. There's a caressing note in his voice, which I find quite amusing. And his behavior..."

Maggie sighed. At least she could tell Karr that his campaign had been successful, so he could cut it out.

Libby sounded intrigued. "Now that's fascinating. The women in the office said—"

Maggie didn't want to hear it, and she'd rather not give Brenda any more ideas. She said firmly, "You'll water my plants, won't you, Libby?"

Libby stared at her for a moment, then took the hint with grace. "Of course. In fact, I've already moved them to my house, because it looks as if I'll be too busy to run out to Eagle's Landing. Not that I won't be spending some time there—"

"Selling town houses," Maggie said flatly.

"No, it's going to be condos, instead. As soon as the site plans are finished, we can start advance sales. Actually, I can't begin just yet, because I've got a lot of studying and tests to get through before I can be licensed. But in the meantime I can help in the office. And even if I'm only typing contracts, I'll be learning." Libby jumped up. "Listen to me. I'd better get busy. Have you finished that list of what you want me to bring?"

Maggie looked at the legal pad on the desk. It was such a short list. She must have missed something important. "It's ridiculous, but I can't think of anything else. Oh, a couple of skirts would help—I'll have to go into the office sometimes, and I can't show up there in a sweat suit."

Libby took the list and the empty suitcase and said goodbye. Maggie watched as Brenda finished putting everything away and finally said, "You know, there's nothing serious about this, really. Between Karr and me, I mean."

Brenda didn't even pause, and her voice was reassuring. "Of course not, dear."

Maggie was startled. Then she replayed Brenda's words in her mind, and realized that she'd been hearing things. Brenda hadn't said anything at all about a romantic attachment, just that she found her son's behavior amusing. It was Maggie's conscience that had filled in the blanks and assumed that Brenda must be thinking Karr was serious.

Maggie started to smile. That was a relief, she thought, and wondered if she should tell Karr he'd underestimated his mother by a mile.

No, she decided. Brenda was right. It *was* pretty funny to watch him.

By Tuesday afternoon, Maggie had finished two more of the main stories for the special edition—except for the fact that the opening paragraph of one of them was so dull she thought no one was apt to read past it and get into the good stuff.

Frustrated, she curled up as best she could on the couch with a printed copy of the story in her lap and started trying out alternative leads. She was just shaping the best one yet when Tripp, who'd been snoozing on the hearth rug, suddenly raised his head, perked his ears inquisitively and leaped up with a peal of barks.

"Thanks for ruining my concentration," Maggie muttered.

It wasn't really Tripp's fault, however, that she'd lost her train of thought. It was what the barks meant that had thrown her off.

Maggie had learned in the past four days to recognize that peculiarly ecstatic noise. She didn't understand precisely how the dog knew that Karr was nearby, but he was never wrong. Since the man showed up at least twice a day, Tripp had had plenty of practice. And, therefore, Maggie had, too.

Thirty seconds later the doorbell rang. Maggie grumbled halfheartedly, put her papers down and hobbled into the hall to answer it.

Karr's hair was windblown, his eyes were bright, and he was wearing a deep red sweater that reflected color into his face.

"You're looking particularly contented with yourself this afternoon," she said.

"I've had a wonderful day." Before she could dodge away, he swept her into his arms and kissed her soundly.

Maggie tried to ignore the way her pulse raced. "That was wasted effort," she said crisply. "Your mother's at the supermarket."

Karr shrugged. "Good quality practice time is never wasted."

"What are you doing here, anyway? It's the middle of the afternoon."

"You don't sound enthusiastic about seeing me."

"I'm not, particularly." Maggie made her voice as blighting as possible. "I certainly don't have time to entertain you. I'm polishing the final draft of a story, and since I've got another progress meeting tomorrow—"

He grinned. "Then it's just as well it isn't you I came to visit, isn't it? I have half an hour to kill, so I thought I'd take Tripp for a run in the park."

"Brenda's already walked him twice today."

"He doesn't look worn out to me, the way he's bouncing around. But of course if all the talk about work is just a bluff and you're trying to convince me to stay with you instead—"

Maggie heaved a melodramatic sigh. "Of course I am. Now you've discovered my darkest secret—that I'm overpoweringly jealous of a six-pound Yorkie." She raised her voice. "Will you just get out of here and stop annoying me? Both of you?"

He laughed and gently tweaked her nose, then retrieved Tripp's leash from the closet. The two of them crossed the street and went into the park.

Maggie picked up her article again. This time she settled down in the window seat at the front of the house. The light was better there, she told herself.

But her eyes kept straying from the typed page to the park, where a tiny dog and a man in a red sweater were wrestling on the grass. She tapped her fingers impatiently on her cast and wished she could be out there, playing with them. As a matter of fact, she realized, she *was* a little jealous.

Tripp was obviously having the time of his life, darting and rushing and playfully nipping. It seemed, lately, as if he was only fully alive when Karr was around....

The room seemed to shift and sway, and something snapped into place deep in her mind like a key bit of a jigsaw puzzle.

You know, she told herself, *the same thing's true of you. You're most alive when Karr is near.*

She didn't understand how or when it had happened. Perhaps it had been when he'd brought her dog safely back to her. Or maybe it had been even earlier—over a pizza, the night the furnace had gone out.

Not that it mattered, of course, precisely when she had fallen in love with him. The fact was, she had—and she might as well stop trying to ignore the truth.

CHAPTER NINE

ONCE the pieces of the puzzle had fallen together, the pattern was clear. The breathless pounding of Maggie's blood every time Karr came near her suddenly made sense, and the restlessness she started to feel when an afternoon slid by and he hadn't shown up yet.

Maggie also understood now why she still hadn't told Karr that his mother was onto his game. She'd kept that secret not because she'd found it amusing to watch his antics and know that Brenda was not deceived, but because she knew if she told the truth, the kisses and touches and hugs would end. And even while she was telling herself that she disliked the attention and the pretense, she'd soaked up the warmth of each moment and hidden it away in her heart.

This revelation even explained why, in the past few days, she had on occasion found the most appalling remarks popping out of her mouth. She had known even as she said those things to him how sharp and unfriendly she must sound—the same way she had sounded a few minutes ago when he arrived.

It wouldn't have hurt her to take a fifteen-minute break and offer him a cup of coffee and a chat. Her work was going better than she'd expected, everything considered. There was something to be said for being tied down with a full-leg cast. But instead of being casually friendly she had snapped at him, made it clear she had no time for him, told him to stop annoying her . . . even though deep inside she had wanted him to stay with her.

153

Now she understood why she'd been so defensive. Her sharp words had been a subconscious attempt to protect herself from another hurt.

She had known how she felt about him, even though she hadn't been able to admit it. And she had known, too, how unlikely it was that Karr could ever feel the same about her. If he had cared in the slightest, he'd have reacted to those cutting remarks with something besides unflagging good humor—a little sarcasm of his own, perhaps, or even anger. But in fact no matter what she said, it seemed that she simply amused him.

Her sharpness had been a double-edged weapon—first a way to test him, and then a defense mechanism. That way Maggie could tell herself that at least Karr hadn't rejected her as Darien Parker had, so cruelly and so long ago, because she had rejected him first.

She could accept being alone, even though solitude was no longer the cure-all she had once thought it to be. She could bear being lonely. But she could not endure being rejected again.

And so she had made her own free choice—subconscious though it was—to drive him away.

Her head was still spinning with sudden self-knowledge when she saw Karr stoop to snap Tripp's leash back on. The man and the dog paused at the curb to wait for traffic before crossing the street, and Maggie hurried away from the window before Karr could catch a glimpse of her.

She was back on the couch when he came in, sorting another stack of manuscripts into piles on the coffee table. "This is still a gigantic mess, you know, and it's all your fault," she muttered. She hardly knew what she was saying herself, but he'd gone to the kitchen and apparently didn't hear.

Maggie sank back against the cushions with relief. Maybe he'd just go on about his business. At least then she'd have some time to think....

A couple of minutes later Tripp bounded in. Karr followed with two tall glasses of lemonade and a plate that held an enormous, thick ham sandwich.

Maggie was startled by the wave of emotion that washed over her as she looked at him. It seemed as though she'd pulled the cork out of a bottle when she'd faced her feelings, and now she was suddenly flooded with all the feelings she'd so carefully denied before—or at least attempted to deny.

Untangling the sensations was trouble enough. There was affection, warmth and tenderness, and of course good old physical attraction—and plenty of it. Her head was buzzing as it did whenever he kissed her. Now, apparently, he didn't even have to touch her to cause the same uproar.

Karr set a glass at her elbow and offered the plate. "I'll share."

She shook her head. "I had lunch. I wouldn't want to steal yours." Her voice was a little rough, and he looked at her oddly.

Maggie almost panicked. She'd be all right, she told herself, once she had some time to adjust to the shock she'd had, to think it all the way through. But what if he could sense what was going on in her head right now?

She looked at the papers in her lap and said, almost automatically, "You might as well have run everything through a shredder, you know."

He put down the half-sandwich he held and said quietly, "I'm sorry I lost my temper and messed up your work, Maggie."

She couldn't look at him. "It's okay. I sort of pushed you into it."

"*Sort of*? Now there's the understatement of the century." The wry note was back in his voice, and Maggie relaxed a little, knowing that he'd been safely distracted, for the moment at least.

She tried not to watch him, but she couldn't quite keep her gaze from sliding away from the manuscripts she was trying to sort and focusing on him instead.

He had sprawled in a big wing chair across the coffee table from her, and he was obviously savoring every bite of the massive sandwich. There was something sensual about his very enjoyment, she thought. But then, Karr seemed to relish everything he did, from petting the dog to kissing her....

He gave Tripp the last couple of bites and told Maggie, "You're watching me as if you're about to give me a lecture on being a freeloader who cleans out my mother's refrigerator the moment her back is turned."

Relieved, Maggie shook her head. "I wouldn't dare. I'm consuming more than my share of Brenda's food budget these days, too." Her hip cramped a little, and she shifted her weight till her cast was stretched out straighter on the couch and her other foot was tucked under her. "And she won't even discuss how I'm ever supposed to pay her back."

"I suspect that's because she plans to let you off the hook and bill me."

"Well, since you're the one who set this arrangement up, and also the one who caused me to fall in the first place—"

"Are you still harping on that? I expect it's going to cost me a packet, too, since she tells me you're an extremely difficult patient."

Maggie was stunned. A difficult patient? But she'd done her best to be cheerful and cooperative, to take care of her own needs and not trouble Brenda with every whim. She'd thought she was succeeding admirably. She'd thought Brenda liked her—

Maggie felt tears sting her eyes and tried to blink them away. Maybe she'd just lived alone so long that she'd forgotten how to act when in close contact with other people. If Brenda thought she was a nuisance—

Her toes were aching, and absentmindedly she tried to rub them. She had to stretch her arm to the limit, and even then it wasn't easy. "Damn," she said vehemently, but she was reacting more to Karr's comment than to the discomfort in her toes.

"You look terribly uncomfortable." He came to sit next to her, picking up her cast and setting it across his lap. The way he positioned the rigid plaster forced her to turn to face him directly.

But Maggie couldn't look him in the eyes. "It's not so awfully bad."

"And I'd say that's a whopper—the very kind of thing Mom was talking about." His fingers curved around her toes, warm and strong and firm as he started to gently rub each one in turn. "She says you're trying to do too much—that you won't let her help you, and you won't even admit when you're in pain."

"Is that her definition of a difficult patient?" Maggie asked hesitantly. "Not that I'm a pest to have around?"

"That's it." Gently but firmly, he began to tug on each toe, massaging the joints. The warmth of his fingers crept through her skin and into the depths of each tiny muscle.

The ache was gone, but the sensation he was creating in its place was every bit as difficult to stand. It was more like slowly creeping fire nudging its way up through her leg.

Karr went on casually, "You've certainly got her fooled."

But not me, he seemed to be saying. *I know what a pain you really are.*

Of course, Maggie thought steadily, she'd never expected him to feel any other way. The fact that she'd had that sudden, blinding revelation didn't mean he'd felt one, too—or ever would. She'd made her reputation with him by being an irritation from the very beginning—she could hardly expect that he'd see her any differently now.

"You can stop," Maggie said. "The ache is gone."

"Am I tickling you?"

"Not exactly, but—"

He didn't stop rubbing, and the way he was looking at her made Maggie nervous. She'd been on edge ever since he'd come in—ill at ease with her new self-knowledge, unsure of where it would lead, half-afraid even to think it through—and at the same time anxious to be alone, so she couldn't slip up and say something that would give her away. If she'd only had a little time to assimilate that new understanding before her self-control had been put to the test...

Karr slid his fingertips under the very edge of the cast to rub the ball of her foot. "How are you getting downtown tomorrow?"

Maggie frowned for a moment before she remembered mentioning her progress meeting. "Brenda said she'd take me."

"Good. I won't have nightmares about you trying to climb the steps at the train platform to take the El."

Sudden warmth welled up in her, and it took effort to keep the tart edge on her voice so he wouldn't suspect how touched she was. "You're afraid I'd fall again?"

"No. I'm afraid you *wouldn't* fall, and then you'd think you were invincible and I'd have you back at Eagle's Landing supervising. Oh, that reminds me." He stopped rubbing long enough to pull an envelope from his hip pocket and hand it to her.

The paper was warm from his body, and Maggie found herself holding it gently, as if it was Karr himself.

"I think it must be the plumber's bill," he said helpfully. "For the time he wasted on your prank call."

Maggie wasn't about to give him the satisfaction of opening it, just in case the balance was shockingly high. She'd worry about that little problem later.

She leaned over the edge of the couch and tucked the envelope into her briefcase. "Are you still going to call it Eagle's Landing?"

"Sure. It's a great name for an upscale commuter complex."

"Libby tells me it's to be condos."

"Did she, now?" Karr's voice was lazy.

Too late, Maggie bit her lip. She'd made the comment absently, without considering that she might be endangering Libby's job before she'd even gotten a fair start. It wasn't exactly a fast track to success to go around talking about the boss's plans.

"I'm sorry if she told me something she shouldn't," Maggie said crisply. "And I assure you I won't pass it on. I was only making conversation, anyway—you're destroying the only thing I have any interest in at Eagle's Landing." It wasn't quite the truth, of course, for anything he did would interest her. But it was the best she could do at the moment to patch up the damage she'd done Libby.

"Oh, I don't blame her for talking. I suspect lots of people say things they don't intend to when they're around you." He glanced at his watch, gave her toes a final rub and stood up, carefully shifting her cast into place on the couch. "Would you like some more lemonade before I go?"

I'm glad he's going, Maggie told herself. She'd wanted him to go, so she'd have a chance to think. Still, now that the moment had come, she didn't feel pleased at all. Part of her wanted to reach up and grab his hand and pull him down to her—but that was ridiculous, of course.

"No, thanks," she said.

Had the fact that she knew about the condos offended him, sending him away earlier than he'd intended? Or had he simply been killing some time—as he'd said he was, she reminded herself—before keeping an appointment?

Both possibilities—that he was irritated with her or saw her as half an hour's worth of distraction—made her feel a little ill.

Karr gathered up his plate and the lemonade glasses and took them to the kitchen. When he returned, he didn't even come into the living room, just leaned against the doorway to say, "I gave Tripp a rawhide chew. That should keep him too occupied for a while to notice I'm gone."

Maggie nodded. She'd picked up her almost-finished story, so she had an excuse not to look at him, and she was making small, meaningless marks all over it.

The front door closed behind him, and a sudden stillness settled over the house. Maggie stopped tracing circles on her paper and told herself firmly that it was idiotic to wonder why he hadn't bothered to kiss her goodbye. The answer was self-evident—his mother wasn't there to see.

And there was absolutely no reason she should feel like crying.

Maggie hadn't worn a skirt in almost a week, and the long, flowing plaid jersey that Libby had brought felt strange. It wasn't long enough to interfere with her crutches, but the unfamiliar sensation of soft fabric swishing around one leg, while the other felt nothing at all, distracted her. Suddenly she was less certain of her balance than she'd been all week, and she wasn't looking forward to negotiating the elevators and the hallways to get to the magazine office.

Brenda tapped on the bedroom door, and Maggie called, "Come in, I just have to brush my hair and put my jacket on." She wrinkled her nose as Brenda appeared. "Don't I look simply elegant in a dressy suit and one rubber-soled shoe?"

"At least you're safer that way. Karr called to say he's on his way over."

Maggie's hands stilled on the hairbrush. But there was no point in letting anyone—especially Karr's mother—guess how much she wanted to see him, so she kept her voice level. "Bad timing that he's coming just as we're leaving, isn't it?"

"Oh, he's going to take you downtown. He phoned a while ago to say he had business in the Loop." Brenda smiled a little. "Or at least he said he did. Isn't he a dear? He knows how much I hate driving into the city, so he's found an excuse in order to save me the trip."

Of course, Maggie thought, and told herself to cut out the wishful thinking before it got her into big trouble. For a minute there, Brenda had made it sound like Karr actually wanted to see Maggie. But the idea of saving his mother the drive—yes, that sounded much more likely than any desire to do Maggie a favor.

It's only a ride, Maggie reminded herself. Certainly Karr wouldn't think it anything special—and if she was wise, she'd pretend it was simply one of the neighbors who was giving her a lift. She finished brushing her hair and slid into the hunter green jacket that matched her eyes.

Karr was waiting in the hall. He stopped petting Tripp, took Maggie's briefcase from his mother and studied Maggie from head to foot. "Nice change," he said.

It was only a casual compliment, but it still brought a glow to her heart that was difficult to damp down. So she clowned a little, trying to hide her reaction. "I must say it's a challenge to accessorize a full-leg cast." She mimicked the elegant turn of a fashion model on the runway, but the pirouette went awry, and she almost went sprawling.

Karr stepped forward to seize her arm, and Maggie gasped as a jolt of pure energy surged through her.

"You can trust me," Karr said. His voice was huskier than ever. "I won't let you fall."

But it wasn't a physical tumble that scared her. And of course Karr had no idea she was thinking of a far more dangerous kind of plunge.

Maggie's heart still hadn't settled to its normal rhythm when the Mercedes reached the expressway and steadily and almost silently began eating up the miles to the center of the city. But then when had she ever had a normal pulse when Karr was around? From that first encounter outside Eagle's Landing, when he'd looked her over like a piece of real estate he wouldn't mind bidding on, her body had reacted automatically any time he'd been within range. How silly of her to have believed for so long that it was only irritation she felt when he was near!

"You're awfully quiet today," Karr said.

Maggie scrambled for an answer before he could start speculating on why she'd gone silent. "I'm just not looking forward to this meeting. After four years in the magazine business, I ought to be used to the committee approach, I suppose, but since I'm working alone to produce this section, all the meetings seem like a waste of time. And with the deadline coming up fast—"

"I thought it was flexible."

Maggie frowned. "Where did you get that idea? Magazine deadlines are the least flexible in the business."

"From you. You told me the longer I annoyed you, the longer your project would take."

"Oh." She'd forgotten making that particular threat, and she was caught flat-footed. "Well—"

Karr was grinning. "So I've caught you fudging the facts, dear?"

She gathered the shreds of her dignity and decided to ignore her slipup. "I expect the meeting will take a couple of hours. But I can always put in half a day just going through my mail, so don't worry if your business takes longer than that."

"I doubt it will."

He didn't volunteer any details, Maggie noticed. "Then I hope I don't keep you waiting."

"Don't hurry. After I've taken care of my errands, I've got the rest of the afternoon and evening free."

Would you like to spend it with me? The thought came so automatically that Maggie had bitten her tongue before she realized she hadn't said it aloud after all. Good thing, too. He was perfectly capable of issuing invitations himself—if he was so inclined.

"It's thoughtful of you to bother with me to save your mother the trouble." There—she'd at least let him know she didn't think it was her personal attractions that had made him offer to help.

"Oh, believe me," Karr said cheerfully, "compared to some of the things I've done for you, this is no bother at all. The magazine's office is in the Metro Tower, isn't it?"

A few minutes later he turned the Mercedes into the tiny courtyard half-hidden beneath the steel and glass Metro Tower on North Michigan Avenue.

"It's not necessary to go all the way in," Maggie said. "I'll hop out right here, and when you come back, just ask the parking valet to call me and I'll come straight down. Thanks for the—''

The Mercedes pulled up beside the valet stand. "And just how do you plan to get your briefcase upstairs?" Karr asked mildly.

"Sling it over my shoulder, the way I always have."

He looked at her quizzically. "I'd be worried the rest of the day that you'd toppled over in the elevator, dropped the briefcase and killed someone."

He got out before she could answer, leaving the door open for the valet, and came around the car to help Maggie.

The moment she stepped into the magazine's headquarters, her coworkers came rushing to exclaim and sympathize. And to admire Karr, Maggie realized, noticing how many of the women who surrounded her were keeping one eye on him. Most of them were reasonably discreet in their appraisal. Carol, on the other hand, stared straight at Karr and said, "Maggie, who's the dishy guy?"

When Maggie gave his name, Carol's eyes narrowed slightly. "Oh, now I get it. No wonder Maggie doesn't want to move—you're Elliot the Gr—"

Maggie cut in neatly. "If you ever want to see that recommendation, Carol..."

Carol blinked and said weakly, "Elliot the landlord. That's right—that's what I meant."

Karr smiled a little and said he'd come back in a couple of hours. True to his word, he was waiting when the meeting broke up. In fact, he was occupying Maggie's chair, his feet propped on the corner of her desk, drinking coffee.

"No wonder you like working at home," he said, standing up as she came in. "This place is busier than a construction zone."

"That's why I liked Eagle's Landing," Maggie pointed out. "Not just anywhere will do. Your mother's house is wonderful—set so far back from the other houses and with only the park across the street."

"I might be able to find you something in the neighborhood."

It was only a casual offer, Maggie knew, and she responded the same way. "Thanks, but I don't think I could mortgage my honor for the kind of money that would cost. And it's dead sure that nothing else I own is worth that much. I'm ready to go if you are, Karr, but my briefcase is still in the meeting room."

Somehow he'd talked the valet into leaving the Mercedes right by the entrance of the parking garage, so they didn't have to stand and wait for it to be brought around. Maggie sank into the deep leather seat with a sigh, and Karr brushed a hand over her hair and smiled at her. "Crutches aren't much fun, are they? We'd better get you home so you can rest."

"I didn't realize how much effort it takes just to be up and around. Karr, it was really lovely of you to go out of your way to take care of me."

He reached across to her and cupped her chin in his palm, turning her face so he could study her. "Hey, you're different today."

"Am I?" Maggie tried to keep her voice casual.

"Yes. You're softer somehow." His hand came up to cup her cheek, and his mouth brushed hers. "Trust me, Maggie," he whispered. "Tell me whatever it is that's bothering you so."

He sounded as if he really cared, and for a moment Maggie trembled on the edge of a chasm, trying to decide whether to leap into the unknown to see what was waiting for her or draw back to something that looked like safety. She could seize the moment, show her feelings and risk a hurt that would last a lifetime. Or she could take the path of least resistance, continue to treat him with the hands-off attitude she'd developed in the past few days— and never know whether they could have had something more.

A horn blared, and slowly he released her. "Guess we'd better move out of the way." He put the Mercedes into gear.

Trust me, Maggie....

She realized abruptly that somewhere along the line she had let go of the last of her resentment over Eagle's Landing. Certainly she still regretted the loss, and that fact would never change. But Karr had made a simple business decision in buying the property, tearing down the house, rebuilding. Even if Maggie couldn't entirely agree with his choices, she couldn't fault him for making them—property development was the way he made his living, after all. And if Karr hadn't seized the opportunity, chances were good someone else soon would have. Libby and Dan were right about that. Eagle's Landing was ripe for development.

Trust me, Maggie. Tell me whatever it is that's bothering you so.

Could she trust him? Could she tell him about her debt and her foolishness... and about Darien Parker?

Karr seemed different today, too. There was no audience now to be impressed by how tenderly he'd cared for her. And if there was ever to be any hope of something between them...

The Mercedes stopped at a traffic light, and suddenly Maggie was looking straight into his eyes—deep blue and questioning. Her world hung in the balance for a moment, then settled into a slightly different orbit.

"Let's go home and call in an order for Chinese," she said. "Brenda's got a club meeting tonight, and we could build a fire... and really talk."

"I'd like that," he said quietly. "My treat."

The decision was made, and she wouldn't back out—
but that didn't erase the disquieting sensation that she
might have done the wrong thing. Maggie found herself
almost chattering, filling time as they crossed the city.

She was talking about Brenda's house as they came
into Eagleton. "You know, I'm surprised you don't appreciate old buildings more. Growing up in that house
must have been an education in architectural appreciation—it's a wonderful example of how an old house
can grow in beauty and value over the years."

"I didn't grow up there."

"Didn't you? I just assumed . . . Well, maybe that ex-
plains it." The Mercedes flashed past the turnoff that
led to Eagle's Landing, and she said hastily, "Karr, I
just remembered—there's another book I need so I can
finish the last article for the issue. Can we stop at
Eagle's Landing and get it? I know it's a bother, but if
you'd run up and get it for me . . ."

He didn't slow down, and the atmosphere in the car
seemed to harden. "Sorry." His voice was clipped and
curt.

Maggie felt as if she'd hit a concrete wall. "But why
not? It'll only take a couple of minutes, and you said
you had all evening free—"

"Can't you borrow it from the library?"

"I doubt I could get it in time. I can tell you exactly
which shelf it's on, Karr. It's no big deal."

Karr sighed. "Yes, it is. With the best will in the world,
I can't get your book, Maggie, because it's not on that
shelf any more."

Her voice was low, level and dangerous. "Where is
it?"

He took a deep breath. "In storage. Everything's
packed up in crates, in the moving company's warehouse, till you decide where you're going. Finding any
one item would be next to impossible."

"You shipped everything off without even asking me?" She was almost shrieking.

"You aren't going to need your pots and pans and chairs for a month or so."

"That is entirely beside the point!"

"As for the other stuff, you had your chance to get anything you needed."

"Oh, right." Maggie's voice oozed sarcasm. "Even though you didn't think to mention what you were up to—"

"All you had to do was tell Libby."

"I had no idea it was a last-chance situation! You said you'd wait."

"What?" Karr sounded honestly puzzled. "I said *what*?"

"You said if I hadn't come back from my trip before the deadline, you'd have waited before you did anything."

"I may have said that when we were still talking about an able-bodied tenant who somehow managed to miss the legal notice. But it made no sense to leave your things there once you were physically out of the apartment. You knew I was going to tear the place down—"

"You said you were going to salvage all the treasures. What's the big deal about leaving the roof on my apartment for a few more weeks?"

The Mercedes pulled up to the curb in front of Brenda's house, and Karr turned the engine off. "I'm not going to hold up my plans so you can have a fancy storeroom for your belongings, if that's what you expected."

She opened the door of the Mercedes. "And you had the gall to ask me to trust you when you didn't even bother to tell me you'd put everything I own into limbo?" Her voice was soft—she was almost choking on the lump in her throat. "Under the circumstances, I think we'll cancel the Chinese food and the fire, so please don't bother to come in."

Karr pulled the keys from the ignition switch with a snap. "Oh, cut out the grand-lady nonsense. Just how do you think you're going to manage without a favor when your crutches are in the trunk?"

She couldn't hide the way she flinched at the sharp edge in his voice, but Karr had already gone around to the back of the Mercedes, and by the time he got her crutches Maggie had herself under control once more.

Silently, he carried her briefcase to the house and unlocked the door while Maggie was still fumbling to find her key. He set the briefcase down and ignored Tripp's ecstatic greeting for the first time all week. "Maggie—"

"Thank you for the ride," she repeated tautly. "It was kind of you to bother."

He said something under his breath. She didn't hear the words, but the fierce tone was enough to tell her she didn't want to know precisely what it was.

He didn't slam the door. She'd have felt better if he had. In fact, she thought about doing it herself, just to release a little strain. If it had been her own instead of Brenda's, she might have done it.

Tripp was standing stock-still in the hall, staring at the front door as if he couldn't believe he'd been ignored by the man he'd come to worship. Then he sat down as if he intended never to move again and began to whine, a low, keening cry that acted like sandpaper on Maggie's nerves.

"You'd better get used to it," she recommended. She limped into the living room. "You won't be seeing much of your hero any more."

But she couldn't help but wonder if she was really talking to the dog—or to herself.

CHAPTER TEN

THE only thing that consoled Maggie was work. For the next two days she buried herself in the special section for as many hours as she could, only stopping to take a break when the eyestrain became too much to bear. She hardly came out of her room except for meals. At least that way, when Karr came to see his mother, Maggie was less likely to encounter him.

But he didn't come.

Maggie could almost see the questions in Brenda's mind, but they remained unasked. Maggie was silently grateful, for how could she possibly explain to Karr's mother that the imaginary romance had been real after all—at least on Maggie's side? She couldn't, that was all, and have any shred of pride or dignity left.

By Friday afternoon, she'd finished reading every unsolicited manuscript and story she'd brought home. Her briefcase was almost empty, but the pile of envelopes waiting to be returned to their authors took up half the surface of her desk. Once she was rid of those, she could cover the desktop with layout sheets and start arranging the stories in order and planning illustrations and headlines. There was still one last story to write, and a good bit of polishing remained to be done to be certain all her work was as professional as possible. But it looked as if she'd be finished at least a week before the deadline.

At least something good had come out of all the pain, she thought, and went in search of Brenda to ask a favor.

Brenda was in the front hall, polishing the elaborately turned spindles that supported the stair rail. Tripp was sitting on a rug just inside the door, his chin propped against the beveled glass sidelight, staring down the walk. He turned his head when Maggie came in, but he didn't get up. He just thumped his tail twice against the marble floor in halfhearted greeting and returned to his melancholy survey of the landscape.

Maggie's heart wrenched at the sight. None of this was Tripp's fault, but he was being punished most of all. If only there was some way to make him understand, she thought.

"Brenda, I wondered if you might be going to the post office in the next few days," she said hesitantly. "I've got a lot of things to be mailed. There's nothing urgent—"

"I'll be happy to take them." Brenda ran her polishing cloth around another baluster. "I have some errands to run, anyway."

"I'll get you some money, just in case the postage isn't right." Maggie started to hobble away, but Brenda stopped her.

"What's wrong, dear? It's plain how unhappy you are. I know you and Karr have quarreled, and you've been avoiding me for a couple of days. If there's anything I've done—"

"No," Maggie gasped. "No, it's not you, it's me. Brenda, I'm going to look for another place to live."

In fact, she'd already started reading the ads—without much success. Her needs had been difficult enough to meet before the accident, but with the cast it would be even tougher to find a place she could manage. Right now, though, she'd take almost anything, just to stop causing Brenda pain.

Brenda's eyes were shadowed. "Aren't you happy here?"

Maggie swallowed hard. "Of course I am. I love you, Brenda, and it's wonderful here. But I'm such a lot of trouble...." Her voice trailed off.

"I know that you feel you are, but it's simply not true. And it's ridiculous to talk of leaving till you're out of the cast and can manage on your own—so let's stop talking nonsense, all right?"

Maggie said, miserably, "Even though Karr won't come back till I've gone?"

"Karr's an adult. I think if he wants to see his mother badly enough, he'll find a way." Brenda gave a baluster a last rub and folded her polishing cloth. "Now where are those things you want mailed?"

With her desk cleared, Maggie started to sketch out how the special section would look. But her mind wandered, and when she pulled herself back, she found Karr's name printed neatly across the center of her layout sheet.

She reached for the telephone before she could talk herself out of it. She'd just leave a message asking him to stop by, she decided, and if he came—well, she'd worry then about what she'd say.

But he was in the office, and before she even had a chance to gather her wits, the receptionist had transferred her call.

"Karr?" she said hesitantly. "It's Maggie. Can you stop by sometime? I'd really like to talk to you."

There was a long silence. "I'll see if I can fit it in."

"This afternoon would be good," she offered. "Your mother's gone for a while. But whenever you can come will be fine."

Her palm was damp when she put the telephone down. Now she just had to wait—and that would be the most difficult thing of all. She'd be on edge all the time, not knowing when he might come. And he hadn't promised, she realized, only said he'd try. She might have to wait days....

But at midafternoon, he rang the bell.

Maggie opened the door and studied him silently for a long moment. There was something about his eyes, darker than usual and fixed intently on her face, that made her tremble inside. And he was more formally dressed than she'd seen him before, too, in gray trousers and a navy sports coat, and a striped silk tie. She hadn't ever seen him wearing a tie.

Tripp gave a hoarse little bark and leaped as high in the air as he could, his tongue swiping madly at Karr's fingers. Karr stooped to pick up the animal and held him easily in one palm, absently stroking his fur with the other hand. "You said you wanted to talk to me," he reminded her.

Maggie nodded and led the way into the living room. She sat on the couch and carefully set her crutches within reach. Karr took the wing chair and arranged Tripp on his knee.

Seeing him here, and remembering the last time they'd been together in this room—when he had so tenderly rubbed the ache from her toes—made the lump in Maggie's throat grow even larger. The only things she could think of were how much she loved him and how much she wanted for him to love her in return.

Her voice was husky. "I told your mother a little while ago that I was looking for another place to go."

Karr's fingers stilled on Tripp's fur. The dog nudged his hand and yipped a little, and the mechanical stroking continued.

Was it relief he was feeling, Maggie wondered. It was impossible to tell. His face was impassive.

"The trouble is there just aren't any other options right now," Maggie went on quietly. "I'll keep looking, of course, and I'll move as soon as I can. But in the meantime, it isn't fair to your mother that I'm keeping you away. So I wanted you to know that you don't have to be afraid of me making a scene or anything. Whenever you come to see Brenda, I'll just go to my room. In fact if you want to call ahead of time, I'll stay out of sight altogether."

There was a long silence. "That's what you called me about," he said levelly.

Though it wasn't a question, Maggie nodded anyway. He sounded almost annoyed, she thought, as if she was wasting precious time with trivia. "That, and Tripp. He's missed you so. This mess isn't his fault, and he doesn't understand why he's being cheated out of his exercise. So I wondered if you'd..." Her voice trailed off. "If you'd take him out once in a while, and gradually get him used to doing without you."

He was looking at her as if he thought she'd gone completely mad. "All right," he said finally. "I don't have time to take him for a run right now, but I'll come back later. Will five o'clock be convenient?"

She nodded. The chilly tone of his voice seemed to freeze her throat completely.

Karr put the dog down and stood up. Maggie followed him to the door, as a good hostess would, trying not to let the tears that stung her eyelids overflow. But her vision blurred just as Tripp danced under her crutch. The rubber tip slipped against the marble, and in a split second Karr was there to steady her, his arm as solid as a steel brace around her waist.

Maggie closed her eyes and tried not to breathe, knowing that the simple tangy scent of his cologne would be enough to dissolve her determination. If he kissed her...

The touch of his lips against her temple was so fleeting that she almost told herself she was imagining it. But his mouth was cold—as cold as the wind outside, as cold as his voice had been. A last and bittersweet kiss...

He was as good as his word. At the stroke of five, he was on the doorstep, casually dressed in khakis and a sweater. As soon as he and Tripp had crossed to the park, Maggie came out of her bedroom and took up a post at the window, taking care to stay behind the curtains. Her conscience tingled a bit at the idea of spying, but she smothered it. After all, she'd never promised that she wouldn't catch sight of him.

He came at least once every day after that, and Maggie kept her promise. But it didn't get easier to go to her room when she saw him coming up the walk or heard Tripp's hearty greeting. Seeing him from a distance only reminded her of how much more she wanted, and how far the remaining weeks stretched out before her cast came off and she would be free.

She started feverishly reading the listings of apartments for rent, hoping desperately to find something that would work. If she rented closer to downtown, she wouldn't have the cost of commuting—but that wasn't the real reason she concentrated on that section of the ads. If she was closer to the office, she would also be farther from Karr—and she wouldn't have to hold her breath every time she went to the supermarket or the office supply store or the train station... or all the other places in Eagleton that now held memories of him.

At mid-morning on Tuesday, Brenda was cleaning flower beds in the back garden and Maggie was stretched on the living room couch with her computer balanced on her lap, doing the final edit on her lead story, when Tripp roused from a snooze in front of the empty fireplace and started barking frantically.

An instant later, she heard the click of a key in the front door, and she looked up in astonishment. She knew Karr had a key—he'd used it the night of their quarrel.

But Brenda had said he seldom used it. Raiding his mother's refrigerator was one thing, she'd told Maggie with a laugh, but he was absurdly sensitive about walking into Brenda's house without ringing the bell.

Hastily, Maggie punched the buttons that would copy her story into the computer's long-term memory and waited impatiently for the screen to clear so she could pick up her work and retreat to her bedroom. It took only a matter of seconds, but by the time she was finished, Karr was in the living room, striding across the deep-piled carpet to stand over her with his hands on his hips.

"Sorry," she said. "If you'll give me a minute, I'll get out of your way." She clicked the computer off and swung her cast down from the couch.

He bent over her and picked her up. The computer slid off her lap and landed with a thump on the carpet.

"Dammit, Karr," Maggie cried, "what do you think you're doing? If you're trying to destroy everything I've worked for—"

"No, I leave that sort of thing to you."

She was too stunned at the ferocity of his voice even to struggle in his arms, and before she realized his intention he'd carried her out to the Mercedes. "I don't want to go anywhere with you," she protested. "I have work to do."

"It'll wait."

"I've told you before I'm tired of all this caveman stuff."

He dumped her unceremoniously into the front seat. "Shut up or I'll find the nearest club and hit you over the head, too."

She struggled upright. "What's this all about?" she demanded.

"Don't tell me you haven't got a clue. You may be a damned good editor but you're a lousy actress." He yanked an envelope off the dashboard of the car and dropped it into her lap. "Here—take a look at this while I go after your crutches."

Maggie maneuvered herself into a more comfortable position. Short of crawling back to the house dragging her cast, she didn't have much choice but to sit there. What had gotten into the man, anyway? After nearly a week of speaking to her only when she'd forced him to, and avoiding her the rest of the time, for him to react like this to some kind of letter—

The envelope was addressed to her, and it had been torn open. That made Maggie's blood really start to boil. Tampering with mail was a federal crime, and by the time she got through with him, Karr Elliot was going to be in such a pile of trouble he wouldn't be able to dig his way out with a bulldozer.

Then she saw the return address—of the historic preservation organization she'd contacted in her abortive effort to save Eagle's Landing—and she winced. She'd completely forgotten that the young man had said he'd send her the group's handbook.

The envelope wasn't very thick—it must be a very small handbook. Well, she thought, if a simple pamphlet about how to set up a neighborhood organization for preserving buildings was enough to make Karr blow his stack like this, maybe it was just as well this relationship hadn't gone any farther.

She slid the contents out of the envelope just as Karr tossed her crutches into the trunk and slammed it.

"Proud of yourself?" he said curtly as he slid under the wheel.

She ignored him. There was a pamphlet folded up inside a letter. She unfolded it, and her eyes widened in shock as she read the first lines. "Thank you for bringing the house known as Eagle's Landing to our attention," the letter began. "While the present level of resources regrettably does not ensure the preservation of every threatened building, from your description Eagle's Landing appears to be a unique, early example of Tudor revival architecture, and we will make every effort to investigate and prevent the destruction of—''

She dropped the letter and whispered, "It's my fault."

"It certainly is," Karr said grimly. He started the engine and pulled away from the curb with a squeal of tires that would have been enough, all by itself, to tell Maggie how angry he was. "Congratulations, Miss Rawlings. You win the prize for discretion. I don't know how you managed it, but I hadn't gotten even a whisper of this."

She took a deep breath. "I didn't manage to keep it quiet, Karr. I didn't know it was going on."

He laughed, harshly. "You expect me to believe that?"

"I admit I started it. I called the preservation people and told them about Eagle's Landing. But they said there are such a lot of threatened houses, and they can't all be saved—and they didn't seem interested in one more old brick house with an unknown architect and a not very exciting past. So I chalked the whole thing up to experience and put it out of my mind, because from what the man at the society said, nothing further was going to happen."

He didn't answer, and he didn't look at her.

Maggie thumped a finger against the letter. "Karr, I'm not an idiot. I know something like this can't be kept secret. When you told me that if there was a hint of opposition you'd knock the house down instead—'' She licked her lips. "Oh, no. Please, Karr, don't do it!"

"But you didn't have to stay involved, did you? You'd set the wolves on me, and you could sit back quietly and enjoy the hunt. What's next? Your tame attorney hitting me with a lawsuit for every penny I'm worth, so I can't fight this?"

She shook her head. Her throat was so tight she couldn't speak. There wasn't any point in further protest, or even in announcing that she'd called Chad Buckley days ago and told him to forget the whole thing.

There would be no persuading Karr to change his mind now. He was taking her out to Eagle's Landing, and he was going to force her to watch as the wrecking ball reduced it to dust and rubble. He'd said he would, and he'd keep his promise....

But instead of turning down the country highway toward Eagle's Landing, the Mercedes sped on across town. Confused, Maggie stared out the window and bit on her thumbnail.

The car stopped in front of the town house sales office, and Karr slammed his door and came around to open Maggie's. "Has it occurred to you that I'd prefer to go in under my own power?" she asked coolly, but he ignored her and picked her up once more.

She could feel the anger still surging through him, but even so, she couldn't help savoring the sensation of being in his arms. She felt tiny and weightless and incredibly feminine as he whisked her up the steps to the small porch and through the door into the office.

The receptionist looked up with a professional smile, which turned to shock as she saw them. Libby turned from the copy machine nearby, and her mouth dropped open. "Maggie? What's going on?"

There was no answer. Karr took the stairs to the upper level two at a time, seemingly unconcerned with his burden. He pushed open a door with his shoulder and put Maggie down in a leather swivel chair at the side of a long table. "Stay put," he said. "I'll be right back."

"As if I could go anywhere," she muttered, but Karr was already gone.

She looked around. The conference room was obviously used for sales meetings. A chart on one wall listed names and figures. A framed set of blueprints hung across from the chart, and nearby on an easel was an architect's perspective drawing of the front of Eagle's Landing.

Before she could study it, Karr was back with a thick manila folder, which he tossed onto the table in front of her. It landed with a thump, and photographs and papers spilled out onto the polished wood of the tabletop.

He leaned over her shoulder and seized a handful of photos. "Here's some of the slate on the roof," he said, thrusting the top picture at her. "Look at how it's crumbling in the valleys. The copper leading's decomposing underneath, too." He picked up a second photo. "Here's what we found when we took the cabinets out of the kitchen."

Maggie gasped at the picture. She recognized the corner, the one where the ceiling had been ripped away—but she hadn't gotten close enough to see the blackened, charred beams above. "That's been on fire!"

"One point for you. Heaven only knows when, but it wasn't fixed, just covered up." He reached for another photograph. "This is what the supports under your bathtub looked like—that's wood rot, in case you don't recognize it. It's a wonder you and a bunch of bubbles hadn't fallen through the floor into a neighbor's apartment."

"Good thing I always took showers, right?"

Karr didn't seem to appreciate the feeble effort at humor. "That big oak tree you were so fond of had cracked the foundation, by the way. One of the basement walls started to collapse last week, and we had to shore it up before we could keep working." With a careless hand, he spread the pictures out in a fan shape in front of her. "Pick a card, any card—you'll see the same sort of thing. On the surface, Eagle's Landing still looked pretty good, everything considered. But underneath—"

Maggie stared at the display. Slowly, she pushed the photographs into a pile, looking at each one in turn, while in the back of her mind a set of gears seemed to grind slowly into action.

This doesn't quite make sense, she thought.

"If it's so obviously not repairable—" she said, and didn't realize for a moment, until Karr seemed to freeze beside her, that she'd said the words aloud.

"Are you questioning my word?" he asked curtly.

"No, Karr, I'm not. These make it pretty obvious." She tapped the pile of pictures and turned her chair so she could look at him. "You shouldn't have any trouble convincing the preservation people. They're not going to waste money on a hopeless cause—there are too many wonderful buildings that still could be saved."

Karr shrugged. "Maybe."

"So—if their interference isn't going to be anything more than a minor glitch in your plans anyway—why are you so terribly upset?" Maggie asked gently. "Why did that letter make you blow a gasket?"

For a long while she thought he wasn't going to answer. Then, without looking at her, he gathered up the photos and slid them into the folder. "I thought you'd given it up," he said quietly. "I thought you understood I wasn't blatantly destroying a landmark just for the fun of it, I was making a business investment."

"I had," she whispered.

He had plunged on. "I thought we were past that sort of incredible blind misunderstanding. I thought we were learning to talk to each other, to trust each other— What did you say?"

"I had, Karr. I'd given up the idea of saving Eagle's Landing, because I respected your judgment, and your right to do what you saw fit. It was yours, after all."

He seemed to have turned to stone.

"I was telling you the truth, before," she went on. "If I'd known what the society was planning to do, why would they have written me that kind of letter, explaining it?"

He didn't answer.

Maggie sighed. He had talked of trust—but obviously that was out of reach now. "That fact doesn't relieve me of responsibility, of course," she said quietly. "I caused this, and I'll do my best to get it sorted out. I'll call the preservation people right away—this afternoon— and tell them what I've seen. I imagine they'd like to look at those photos, at least, but I don't think it will be any problem." She held up a hand in a pledge. Her fingers shook a little. "And then I swear, Karr, I will never interfere in your business again."

A deadly sort of quiet filled the room, interrupted only by the tick of an unseen clock.

Karr said quietly, "I'll take you home."

And that's it? she wanted to scream. *You'll take me home and that's the end?*

But of course it was. She'd been nothing but a nuisance to him all along. Was it any wonder the only thing he seemed to want was to be rid of her as soon as possible? It was unrealistic even to hope for anything else.

She pushed her chair around. "Perhaps you'd be kind enough to get my crutches now? I'd really rather walk than—" Her eyes fell once more on the easel and the perspective drawing it held. Perhaps he would let her have a copy of that drawing, as a memento of Eagle's Landing. Not that she needed a reminder, exactly, but...

She made up her mind to ask, but before the question was formed, she realized the drawing wasn't Eagle's Landing, after all, but some other, eerily similar Tudor revival house.

Karr bent to pick her up, but Maggie held him off with a hand firmly planted against his chest. "Karr, what's that?"

He looked over his shoulder. "Just a drawing of something that doesn't exist. I didn't realize it was in here."

Maggie could feel the steady beat of his heart through her fingertips, pressed against his shirt. The rhythm resounded all the way up her arm. "Just an imaginative drawing?" She was vaguely dissatisfied with the explanation. "There must have been some reason for making it."

"We do that sort of thing all the time."

She wasn't listening. "It looks like a miniature Eagle's Landing."

"You could call it that." He turned away from her as if to study the drawing himself, and rubbed a hand across the back of his neck as if it hurt. "It doesn't matter now, so why not tell you? It's the house I was going to build for you."

She couldn't feel his heartbeat anymore, and it seemed as if her own had stopped cold.

"I was going to take the best of Eagle's Landing," he said softly, without looking at her, "and put it back together for you, solider and better and just the right size...."

I was going to, he'd said. He wasn't talking about now.

"The right size for us," he said, and smiled without humor. "It just goes to show, doesn't it, what a fool a man can be? At first all I wanted was to be rid of you. You were costing me time and effort and money and frustration."

The lump that had formed in Maggie's throat grew larger.

"And then you started costing me sleep and breath and peace of mind. Because, you see, I enjoyed you—

sparring with you, outmaneuvering you, kissing you—more than I've ever enjoyed any woman.''

Maggie stopped breathing. She seemed to have forgotten how.

''I thought the way we struck sparks off each other was no accident. I didn't see how I could be wrong about something so basic. But you didn't care, did you? You didn't want me around. You actively avoided me whenever you could. You even asked me to call before I came to Mother's house so you wouldn't have to see me—''

She shook her head. ''No,'' she whispered. ''I cared, Karr. I cared too much, and I was so afraid. I've always been alone, you see, all my life—even when I was surrounded by other people. And I was terrified that you didn't want me, and that if I let myself care for you I'd be even more alone—''

''No,'' he whispered against her lips. ''I won't let that happen, Maggie, my love. Not now. You will never be alone again.''

She smiled a little. ''It didn't work, anyway,'' she admitted. ''Because I fell in love with you—''

And then there was nothing more to say, with words at least.

It was a long time later when he spread the floor plans out on the table and guided her through her new home, to be built on a lot he owned near Brenda's house. ''It was your idea, really,'' he said.

''Mine? I never dreamed of such a thing—''

''When you suggested that I remodel it and move in myself, I starting thinking of the possibilities. Not of saving Eagle's Landing—I knew when I bought it that wouldn't be possible. But we could have the best of it, on a much more practical scale—the brick and slate, the oak floors and French doors and mantels. Even a top-floor office for you, so you'd have your treehouse again—''

Maggie was almost crying.

"With all the bookcases you can use, and a gas log to curl up beside while you work, under the mantel we took out of your apartment. It's in a warehouse downtown," Karr said, "along with the kitchen cabinets and that grapevine frieze, waiting till we need them." He held her a little distance from him. "Will you mind living in the town house in the meantime? It's going to take a long while to build the Eagle's Nest, I'm afraid."

"The Eagle's Nest," Maggie whispered, and smoothed the worried lines from his forehead with a gentle fingertip. "I'd live in a real nest, or in a tent, or in a condo, with you."

"What *do* you have against condos?"

"A deal that went wrong, a long time ago. It's nothing too important—not any more."

"Is that why you're so conscious of money?"

She nodded. "I was foolish, and I got burned."

"I knew it had to be something like that. Was it silly to want you to trust me enough to confide in me?"

She smiled at him. "No. I think it's wonderful. And I'll tell you all about it—now, or whenever you like."

"Later, then," he said. "I've got better ideas for now."

After he'd finished kissing her, Maggie put her head on his shoulder and looked at the drawing once more. "It's a big job. Can you pull it off, Karr? Because you don't have to, to prove you love me."

"Of course I can pull it off. I've done it before."

She frowned. "I know you renovated the old warehouse into the apartment block," she said, "but that's really not the same."

"This will be easier, in a way, than Mom's house was. She'd picked up pieces from all over creation, and fitting them together was really a jigsaw puzzle. At least I know right now what I've got to work with."

She blinked in surprise. "You built Brenda's house?"

"Yes. That wonderful example of how an old house can grow in beauty and value, I think you said it was." His tone was teasing.

Maggie sighed. "I guess I still have a lot to learn about your business."

"I thought you weren't ever going to interfere in it again."

"I won't interfere, exactly, I'm just interested in—"

Karr gave a whoop of laughter, picked her up and swung her gleefully around the room.

"In everything you do," Maggie finished firmly.

His eyes lighted. "Everything?" he said against her lips, and kissed her until she was too breathless and dizzy to do anything but cling to him, and agree.

UNLOCK THE DOOR TO GREAT ROMANCE AT BRIDE'S BAY RESORT

Join Harlequin's new across-the-lines series, set in an exclusive hotel on an island off the coast of South Carolina.

Seven of your favorite authors will bring you exciting stories about fascinating heroes and heroines discovering love at Bride's Bay Resort.

Look for these fabulous stories coming to a store near you beginning in January 1996.

Harlequin American Romance #613 in January
Matchmaking Baby by Cathy Gillen Thacker

Harlequin Presents #1794 in February
Indiscretions by Robyn Donald

Harlequin Intrigue #362 in March
Love and Lies by Dawn Stewardson

Harlequin Romance #3404 in April
Make Believe Engagement by Day Leclaire

Harlequin Temptation #588 in May
Stranger in the Night by Roseanne Williams

Harlequin Superromance #695 in June
Married to a Stranger by Connie Bennett

Harlequin Historicals #324 in July
Dulcie's Gift by Ruth Langan

Visit Bride's Bay Resort each month wherever Harlequin books are sold.

Yo amo novelas con corazón!

Starting this March, Harlequin opens up to a whole new world of readers with two new romance lines in SPANISH!

Harlequin Deseo
- passionate, sensual and exciting stories

Harlequin Bianca
- romances that are fun, fresh and very contemporary

With four titles a month, each line will offer the same wonderfully romantic stories that you've come to love—now available in Spanish.

Look for them at selected retail outlets.

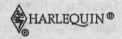 HARLEQUIN ®

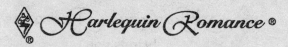

Harlequin Romance ®

New from Harlequin Romance a very special six-book series by

MIDNIGHT SONS

DEBBIE MACOMBER

The town of Hard Luck, Alaska, needs women!

The O'Halloran brothers, who run a bush-plane service called **Midnight Sons**, are heading a campaign to attract women to Hard Luck. *(Location: north of the Arctic Circle. Population: 150—mostly men!)*

"Debbie Macomber's *Midnight Sons* series is a delightful romantic saga. And each book is a powerful, engaging story in its own right. Unforgettable!"

—Linda Lael Miller

TITLE IN THE MIDNIGHT SONS SERIES:

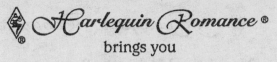

Harlequin Romance ®
brings you

How the West Was Wooed!

We've rounded up twelve of our most popular authors, and the result is a whole year of romance, Western style. Every month we'll be bringing you a spirited, independent woman whose heart is about to be lassoed by a rugged, handsome, one-hundred-percent cowboy! Watch for...

- April: A DANGEROUS MAGIC—Patricia Wilson
- May: THE BADLANDS BRIDE—Rebecca Winters
- June: RUNAWAY WEDDING—Ruth Jean Dale
- July: A RANCH, A RING AND EVERYTHING—Val Daniels
- August: TEMPORARY TEXAN—Heather Allison

HITCH-3

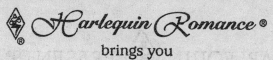

Harlequin Romance ®

brings you

Some men are worth waiting for!

They're handsome, they're charming but, best of all,
they're single! Twelve lucky women are about to
discover that finding Mr. Right is not a problem—it's
holding on to him.

In April the series continues with

#3406 THE RIGHT KIND OF MAN
by Jessica Hart

Skye had run away from man trouble, only to bump
smack into Lorimer Kingan. He was tall, dark and
handsome, and he wanted an efficient, reliable PA.
Skye desperately wanted the job, but could she really
describe herself as *efficient*? Worse, she knew as soon
as she saw him that Lorimer was the right kind of
man for her!

Hold out for Harlequin Romance's heroes in
coming months…

- May: MOVING IN WITH ADAM—Jeanne Allan
- June: THE DADDY TRAP—Leigh Michaels
- July: THE BACHELOR'S WEDDING—Betty Neels

HARLEQUIN PRESENTS®

The latest in our tantalizing new selection of stories...

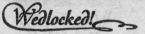

Bonded in matrimony, torn by desire...

Next month watch for:

Ruthless Contract by Kathryn Ross
Harlequin Presents #1807

Locked in a loveless marriage. Abbie and Greg were
prepared to sacrifice their freedom to give Abbie's adorable
nieces a stable home...but were determined that their
emotions wouldn't be involved.

Then fate stepped in and played her final card, and
the ruthless contract between Abbie and Greg became a
contract for passion.

Available in April wherever Harlequin books are sold.